D0834999

THE UNKNOWN HUNTSMAN

Jean-Michel Fortier

THE UNKNOWN HUNTSMAN

*Translated from the French
by Katherine Hastings*

QC FICTION

Revision: Peter McCambridge
Proofreading: Riteba McCallum, David Warriner
Book design and ebooks: Folio infographie
Cover & logo: YQB MÉDIA
Fiction editor: Peter McCambridge

Copyright © 2014 by La Mèche
Originally published under the title *Le chasseur inconnu*

Translation copyright © Katherine Hastings

ISBN 978-1-77186-082-6 pbk; 978-1-77186-083-3 epub;
978-1-77186-084-0 pdf; 978-1-77186-085-7 mobi/pocket

Legal Deposit, 4th quarter 2016
Bibliothèque et Archives nationales du Québec
Library and Archives Canada

Published by QC Fiction
6977, rue Lacroix
Montréal, Québec H4E 2V4
Telephone: 514 808-8504
QC@QCfiction.com
www.QCfiction.com

QC Fiction is an imprint of Baraka Books.

Printed and bound in Québec

Trade Distribution & Returns
Canada and the United States
Independent Publishers Group
1-800-888-4741 (IPG1);
orders@ipgbook.com

Société
de développement
des entreprises
culturelles
Québec 🔲🔲

We acknowledge the support from the Société de développement des entreprises culturelles (SODEC) and the Government of Quebec tax credit for book publishing administered by SODEC.

Financé par le gouvernement du Canada
Funded by the Government of Canada | Canadä

We acknowledge the financial support of the Government of Canada through the National Translation Program for Book Publishing, an initiative of the Roadmap for Canada's Official Languages 2013-2018: Education, Immigration, Communities, for our translation activities.

1

WE MEET ONCE A WEEK in the big parish hall beneath the church, the parish hall whose walls are steeped in sin, with its low ceiling as though it had been flattened by something bigger. Because of course when it comes to religion, it's all about size. We meet there the day after the Lord's day. A big gathering on Sunday in the church, all white and clean, cold and vast as the heavens, then another smaller meeting in the dark, dingy, hot-as-hell basement on Mondays. We often think what a shame it is that mass isn't held in the parish hall too because, for napping, nothing beats a warm room, as I'm sure you'll agree.

It's not the priest who runs the Monday meetings. He sits on a metal chair like the rest of us mortals. On Mondays, everyone's an equal and, believe us, it's a good thing, what with the baker who thinks he's mayor and the mayor who often thinks he's God, and then the priest with all his connections, it would be a right mess.

Most of the time, nobody says anything for a good fifteen minutes. We rub the back of our necks, look down at the floor, then up at the ceiling, for good measure. Often a woman will pipe up first, grumbling about something or other, like last week when Angelina White complained about the ruckus caused by the children of Lisa Campbell, the hairdresser, who allows her brood to run wild in the street until all hours, then lets them loose again in the morning before Farmer McDonald's rooster has even thought about crowing:

"My sole concern is for the health of the little ones. Mrs. Campbell, children simply cannot thrive on three or four hours' sleep a night. It's not good for them."

When the accuser is a woman as virtuous as Angelina White, the affair is wrapped up in no time, and the show of hands is conclusive: we ask Mrs. Campbell to control her children, *e basta*. The *e basta* is a little Italian twist, at the request of Giorgio Cantarini, the war widower whose wife died at the laundry—boiled to death—while he was at the front, and it was also with a show of hands that we had voted to always wrap things up with *e basta*.

There's something definitive and faintly exotic about it, we think, except for Cantarini, that is, who still speaks the language and, as a matter of fact, it took us ages to understand what he meant by *e basta* anyway because he didn't even bother asking us in our own language. We've since taught him the basics of the language, and now he can get by in society.

Once the first complaint has been aired, often by a prim and proper lady, the ice is broken and we can all speak openly. Every now and again a man will stand up and make a minor—or sometimes major—announcement, like last month when Albert Miller shared his intentions:

"I'm going to marry Blanche Bedford."

The would-be bride was not in attendance, as she had yet to turn eighteen, the minimum age for taking part in the Monday meeting. Not because matters of a particularly adult nature were discussed there, but rather because if it weren't for the rule, Mrs. Campbell would bring along her flock of children, and there's simply not enough room for them to tear around in there. The age limit is another decision we made together, but of course we never let on that it was to keep out the Campbell kids. That would have irritated their mother no end, and our Monday meetings aren't about irritating people; Sunday mass fills that role just fine.

After the announcements, it's time to get down to brass tacks. Very often it's the baker, Mr. Leaven, who gets the ball rolling because, while the Monday meetings are supposed to put us all on an equal footing, the baker is, after all, still the baker, and this one's a real talker, and never at a loss for topics. He plucks a subject out of thin air:

"Stray dogs..."

"The price of flour..."

"Sybille..."

This week, sure enough, he brings up Sybille. You could say she's a recurring theme with him, probably because the baker lives in the last house on St. Andrew's Street, the last one before the forest, the same forest where Sybille spends most of her time. You could practically call it her home, but no one really knows if she actually lives anywhere, in the true sense of the word.

All we know is that she's older than us and she speaks a strange language. Sometimes she cries out at night in her barbarian dialect, and it's as if the entire forest had awoken and was calling for help, and we can sympathize, because Sybille is quite a number. Just ask the baker.

"Sybille has been stealing my loaves, I swear it."

We let out a collective gasp, as never before at the Monday meeting has anyone accused another of stealing, except for the time when Mayor Morton claimed that young Amelia Gross was stealing pens from his desk although, after an investigation into the matter, we realized they'd simply rolled into the heating vent under his desk, where they slowly melted, which explained why the village office smelled like scorched ink for the longest time, but in any case, Mayor Morton was relieved of his duties because accusing someone without proof is just not done, well, actually it is, but not when you hold office. So we sent Morton packing, and he killed himself shortly after, who knows if the two events were connected, and we elected Amelia's father, Roger Gross, who is still our sitting mayor. We probably did so partly to right the wrong done to his child, after all, who would want a Gross as mayor, but at least he never goes around pointing fingers, and his daughter is happy now, except for when she claims to anyone who will listen that she won't live a day beyond the age of fourteen. God only knows where she got such an idea, but come to think of it, we wonder whether it could have been Sybille, speaking of whom, here goes the baker again about his missing loaves:

"Every evening I prepare my bread before I go to bed, around nine o'clock. That way, I can sleep in a bit longer and all I have to do is bake the loaves before I open up at eight the next morning."

That's our baker, we think. Always sleeping and dreaming about his bed—or about a woman in his bed—with his fat belly stuffed full of dough. We suspect he eats more bread than he sells and, according to his neighbour, the florist, who swears she heard him one July evening, his yeasty belches resound for hours at a time, but Leaven hasn't finished:

"For the past two weeks, I've set my loaves out on the windowsill in the evenings between 8:30 and 8:45 to air them out a bit. I figure it can't do them any harm to feel the spring breeze. It's important to let the bread breathe, you see.

But I noticed that yesterday—and last Friday too—there were two loaves missing when I went to collect them. Because, you see, I always set one dozen loaves on the sill and yesterday, when I went to get them, there were only ten."

While we find his story plausible enough, we wonder whether he counted them properly before laying them on the windowsill, but we soon discard the idea of an error on his part: the baker is good with numbers, and if he says he made twelve loaves, there's no way he made only ten. There's no doubt about it; the man knows how to count. All the same, to err is human, but before we can decide whether to raise the possibility, the baker continues:

"And that's not all. Yesterday when I went to get my bread, there on the sill, where there should have been two loaves, were two small clay bowls full of wild strawberries."

We gasp in unison, because we know full well there's only one person around who makes such bowls to carry her wild strawberries in, the only person who doesn't own a single plastic container—not that we've never offered her any. It's just that she prefers to live that way, like an Indian, like a savage, as we say, anyway as you've probably guessed by now, the person we're talking about is, of course, Sybille, who the baker is accusing ever more blatantly of breadlifting, and he could well have a point.

"Do you see? It's as if she paid me for the bread with wild strawberries. But the problem is—and here I'm talking to you, Mr. Mayor and Father Wavery—a loaf of bread is worth far more than a handful of strawberries that I can pick myself just outside my own bakery door. It's not as if it's a fair exchange."

Our gaze shifts to Mayor Gross because, between him and the priest, it's the mayor who has the final say on financial matters, of course it should probably be up to a judge to decide, but there is no judge in the village, and even if there were, who knows whether he'd even attend the Monday meetings. Rumour has it that judges only leave their chambers for professional visits, that they call their mothers once a year on All Saints' Day and that's it, so why shouldn't Mayor Gross decide whether or not Sybille is guilty, even if she's not here to defend herself. She's probably up to no good in the woods or perhaps she's stealing from one of the villagers at this very instant, which reminds us we're going to have to keep a close eye on our belongings from now on, a thief in our midst—who could have imagined such a thing?—and now the mayor looks like he wants to say something:

"M-m-my friends. B-b-baker L-l-l-leaven. Un-un-unfounded a-a-accusations are n-n-n-not w-w-w-welcome here. Re-me-me-member my d-d-d-daughter Amelia and the b-b-business with the pens."

We forgot to mention that Mayor Gross has an awful stutter, another strike against him in addition to his unflattering name, who would have thought that a stutterer with a name like his would one day become mayor? His mother must be proud but, never mind, let's hear what else the mayor has to say:

"I-I-I think it's b-b-b-est to stick to the facts. M-m-mister L-l-leaven, I w-w-will investi-ga-ga-gate this b-b-b-read theft my-my-myself. F-f-f-first thing to-to-tomorrow."

Mayor Gross is not the kind of man who rules with an iron fist, as you've probably noticed; Mayor Morton, on the other hand, now *he* knew how to run a tight ship, unfortunately he had a tendency to accuse children of stealing, and that's an unfortunate habit for a politician, ahh, there's Father Wavery getting to his feet, that's unusual for him—he usually just sits there in the corner and scratches his nose.

"My children, let us all go home now. There's no point continuing to badmouth one another. Let's all just sleep on it."

They seem to want to cut the meeting short. We notice the priest is sweating more than usual, perhaps he has an upset stomach this evening, or maybe it's nerves. We don't dare ask; a holy man's intestinal health is between him and God, but at least the meeting hasn't dragged on forever, and now we can go home and keep an eye on our things, oh yes, we're going to keep our eyes peeled from now on.

2

WE MEET EVERY FRIDAY in the church basement, Fridays because that's the only evening everyone is at home, relaxing quietly by the fire. They cherish their habits in the village. We're always a little worried we'll get caught. On Mondays they hold the village meeting right here in the same hall. Ironic, isn't it? They come to air their petty problems while we...

The Professor raises his finger.

"My brothers and sisters, welcome!"

He always begins with that. It reassures us. We smile.

"My children, you may have attended the Monday meeting and heard the accusations made against one of ours."

We shudder. The Professor rubs his gold-rimmed glasses and thunders:

"This is a cowardly act! Oh so cowardly! Weak is he who accuses without proof. Remember Morton and his ridiculous ideas about the daughter of one of our members..."

Morton, that idiot. He paid dearly for his treachery.

"That's right, on Monday they accused Sybille of stealing."

A quiver of fear runs through us.

"Sybille, a pilferer... can you believe it!"

He gives us a mischievous look and bursts into raucous laughter. We look at each other and titter softly. The Professor knows how to calm our nerves.

"And you know what the funniest thing is? Do you know what she is accused of stealing?"

We hang on his every word.

"Bread! Oh, but not just any bread... *Loaves*, to be precise!"

He spreads his arms and legs wide and skips across the stage. And now we really can't con-

tain ourselves, we double up with laughter, guf-
fawing until tears run down our cheeks.

"I ask you," he goes on. "What on earth would
Sybille want with loaves of bread?"

By this time, we're rolling on the floor in hys-
terics, banging our palms and feet on the lino-
leum, we've never heard anything so hilarious.

"No, I mean, seriously, I'm asking you!"

We can't stop laughing, what a wonderful
sense of humour he has!

"I'm asking you!"

Our ribs ache, our eyes stream with tears of
joy, what a resounding success this meeting is
turning out to be!

"I'm asking you, I said I'm *asking* you!"

A loud crack rings out from the front of the
hall as a pane in one of the basement windows
shatters. We look up. The gun in the Professor's
hand is still smoking.

"I said I'm asking you!"

He is furious. He hates it when we don't do
as he says. When he asks a question, he expects
an answer. How stupid we are, how ashamed we
feel. We raise our hand, our arm trembles and
we grip it tight with the other hand.

"Yes? What is it?"

"Professor, you wish to know what Sybille would do with loaves of bread, is that right?"

Our voice quivers slightly. He stares at us through his fogged-up gold-rimmed glasses. We've only got one chance; we must get the answer right.

"Perhaps she could eat them?"

The Professor points his gun straight at us. We cover our face with our hands. In a nearly inaudible voice he asks:

"Eat them?"

We tremble.

"Eat them, have I heard you correctly?"

We nod, we think we may faint. Centuries pass. It's amazing how a metal pipe levelled at you can freeze the blood in your veins.

He finally turns his gun away. He gazes at us for a long time, then gales of laughter burst forth from his mouth.

"Eat them!"

We smile. We're pleased he likes our suggestion. He laughs even harder.

"Eat them! You'd think I was surrounded by a bunch of retards. Hah! Eat them!"

We're in heaven. The Professor has found a name for us. We're now worthy of a name. We are "retards." This meeting has been truly

wondrous. He whoops uproariously and won-
derfully, then becomes serious again:

"But the fact remains, that baker is a real
scourge. Always has been. One of these days
we'll have to do something about him. Now go
home, my children. You need to rest. We'll have
to see how this business with Sybille plays out."

Our Professor motions to one of the plumper
members among us and walks her to the back of
the hall, how lucky she is! A private conversation.

We leave the hall, blissful, just as the rain
begins to drum down, seeping in through the
broken windowpane.

3

DESPITE WHAT THEY SAY, that human nature takes a thousand and one ever-changing forms that would be impossible for us to explain, but— do you hear that?—there we go philosophizing, rambling on, holding forth; Mr. Timothy Worne would be proud, that poor man who struggles daily to capture the interest of his class of ten pupils, though you have to admit the Campbell kids, in particular, aren't easy to control, in fact just last month the middle boy nearly set fire to his desk playing with firecrackers. Amelia, the Gross child, and that bumpkin Bertha, Farmer McDonald's daughter, could set the young thug on the straight and narrow: those two snot-nosed urchins are serious and hardworking at school, and while poor old Bertha will never see much beyond the rabbit hutches of the family farm, Amelia Gross could well end up pursuing an education someplace else, at an institution where she broadens her horizons and gets away from it all, somewhere over the hills and far away, if you get our drift.

But as we were saying, human nature never ceases to amaze, especially in this village, where meetings blend one into the next, although never in quite the same way.

This week Mayor Gross has dragged along his wife Morosity, who in turn has brought her sister, Albania, Amelia's aunt, who we rarely see at meetings, at least not since the time her niece was entangled in the saga of the stolen pens. During that time, Albania never missed a meeting, because if there's one thing you should know about her, aside from her serious thyroid problem, it's that she's as loyal as a dog and she'd throw herself into the well at the end of St. Andrew's Street for her dear Amelia. Her husband, Meaney the apothecary, well, he's another story: he'd sell his mother and father for a pot roast, and rumour has it the reason the two never had children is that Albania used to have night terrors in which her husband would trade their future offspring for three strands of pearls, and even though Doctor Harmer has explained a thousand times that Mrs. Meaney's thyroid causes her terrible suffering, and that a woman needs a healthy thyroid gland to procreate, we're not fooled for a minute. And anyway, Agnes Letterly, the librarian, is well read on the subject and assures us her thyroid is not to blame, that it's actually Mr. Meaney's manic greed that prevents Albania from giving wholly and selflessly of herself, why, he would rob her of everything—even her thyroid—if he thought it would turn him a profit.

But, back to the matter at hand. If you had told us that Morosity Gross would foist her sister Albania on us at the meeting this evening, we would have laughed in your face and spit in your direction, because that's the treatment we reserve for liars in this village. And yet there she is in her enormous flowery dress and curlers— what was she thinking?—it takes an apothecary's wife to go out in public looking like that, and now Morosity is inviting her to sit in a place of choice, the one usually occupied by Mrs. Latvia who, visibly struck to the core, opts to play the martyr and takes the worst seat in the hall, just behind Angelina White, next to a window with a missing pane; now that's odd, we could have sworn it wasn't broken last week.

Father Wavery nods to indicate the meeting is now called to order. As usual, some woman or other is the first to address the gathering to gripe about something or other, and this week, to no one's surprise, because she hates to go unnoticed, it's Albania Meaney who leaps out of her chair to take centre stage in front of the priest:

"Good evening, everyone. I know I haven't been much in attendance at our little meetings recently, but believe me when I say it's not that I don't have the interests of this village at heart; it's my thyroid, you see, that's causing me no end of grief. Oh dear, my poor thyroid..."

She continues on in her annoyingly reedy voice, we can sense Leaven, the baker, shifting impatiently on his chair behind us, he won't stand for this thyroid nonsense much longer, he's never had much time for Albania, and he's happily occupied the spotlight in recent months while she's been convalescing at home, but now he's got some competition in the headstrong department, and if Mrs. Latvia took one of her little pick-me-ups beforehand, we can guarantee there's going to be nearly as much action here tonight as there is on a Saturday night at Old Man George's tavern, but let's get back to Albania, whose soliloquy, with any luck, is drawing to a close:

"... some relief from my poor thyroid, but I'm not here to talk about that."

"I'll give her something to moan about, her and her thyroid."

The baker is losing patience, it's a good thing he muttered under his breath, otherwise things could turn ugly, especially since Lisa Campbell, the hairdresser, hasn't exactly held Albania in her heart either since she started setting her own curlers, but what do you expect when Meaney the apothecary holds the purse strings, it's a lost cause: his wife could have a nest grafted to her scalp and he still wouldn't give a damn, so long as it saved him a penny or two.

"The reason I'm here tonight—just this once, you understand, because I'm barely able to stand—is out of a sense of duty."

Morosity Gross offers her a chair, but Albania ignores it, clutching her throat with one hand while she plumps her curlers with the other like a real drama queen. Rumour has it she was once part of a theatre troupe, that she was an accomplished actress and that the only reason she's languishing in this village is out of love for Meaney, but who knows, that's likely just gossip spread by a bored old woman by the name of Latvia.

"I accuse."

A shiver of excitement runs through us, even timid Angelina White sits up straight; we haven't often heard such words down here, of course last week the baker may have reignited a flame that had been extinguished since the Morton affair with the pens, but since Albania Meaney was still bedridden at our last meeting, we trust she realizes that to accuse another in this village is to play Russian roulette with the odds fully stacked against you.

"I accuse."

What a sense of drama that woman has, and there go Leaven and Lisa Campbell rolling their eyes, and she'd better spit it out and accuse someone pronto, or she's going to be given a thrashing, we're sure of it.

"Is that so, Mrs. Meaney? And who, exactly, are you accusing? Because some of us have bread to bake."

Albania stands erect, taut as a crossbow, her eyes gleaming, and looks straight at the baker:

"I accuse you, my dear man."

If we'd been drinking a cup of tea, we would have gagged and spluttered it all over the back of Morosity Gross's head, well we'll be damned—to accuse someone at the Monday meeting, okay, we've seen it before, but to accuse the baker, now there's a first, and perhaps not the last, in our opinion. She has no idea what she's getting herself into, that Albania—or does she?

Leaven scoffs loudly, no surprise there, his already considerable contempt for Mrs. Meaney has just reached an all-time high:

"You're accusing me. Me? Of what, my dear lady?"

We warned you, a Greek tragedy is about to unfold right before our eyes, poor Angelina White, her chaste ears are sure to transform into cauliflowers and she'll turn as red as a beet, and what about Father Wavery, a man of the cloth, and all the others, and we, who abhor dissension, well, we've seen it all tonight, we would have been better off staying at home and enjoying a nice cup of chamomile tea by the fire, oh the nerve of that Albania Meaney, spoiling our meeting, and she's off again:

"I accuse you of damaging this church that my husband and I fund at our great expense!"

At great expense, that's laying it on a bit thick, Meaney the apothecary never does anything at great expense, least of all charity, even for a church, really, if she thinks she's going to convince us with that argument, she's barking up the wrong tree, we glance around and everyone else seems to be thinking the same thing, what a waste of time, why is it that our meetings must always start this way, Albania clearly hasn't changed, she bangs on the table like a judge and shouts:

"Silence!"

We calm down, Mrs. Latvia knits her brow, and Angelina White fishes a mint out of her handbag.

"I haven't finished."

Albania finally deigns to take the seat her poor sister has been proffering her for the past two centuries, crosses her legs, and launches into what's sure to be a never-ending story.

"In the beginning, I was young and beautiful. I was the envy of all the Mrs. Latvias of this world, this was before I was married."

Mrs. Latvia, who does not take kindly to any references to her advanced age, shifts in her seat and clears her throat. Albania Meaney, in appallingly bad taste, gives her a wink and carries on.

"Then I met Jack (Meaney, her tightwad of a husband), fell madly in love, and settled here, where you all welcomed me so warmly."

Her eyes glaze over and she lifts her index finger and traces a heart in the air, then continues her tale, this time a little hesitantly:

"Anyway, I won't bore you with all the details, but last Friday as I was going out to pick up my thyroid potion at my husband's shop, I bumped into Mr. Leaven, baker by trade, near the church. You know, just in front of the statue of the Virgin Mary and Child who looks so much like me... Then on my way back home, I passed by the church square again and I noticed a pane in that (she points to it) window was broken."

She clutches her throat with both hands in her oh-so-precious, oh-so-Albania pose and the baker stands up and says in a surprisingly calm voice:

"I didn't see you near the church on Friday."

"That's beside the point, Mr. Leaven. Were you at the church square on Friday evening?"

"Yes I was, but I didn't see anyone."

Albania Meaney raises her hand as if to interrupt him and we sense Leaven's hackles rise at the arrogance of this woman in curlers as she leans forward, squints, her hand still raised, and replies:

31

"But you were there."

Then she addresses us all, arms wide open, palms up in a Christ-like gesture:

"He was there."

"You don't have a shred of proof against him. And in any case, no one saw *you* leaving your home. This is utter nonsense. It's worse than the baker accusing Sybille of stealing his bread last week."

It's Mrs. Latvia speaking now. For her to side with the baker, she must be terribly annoyed, bored, or perhaps under the influence of her medication; our eyes widen, now it's two against one, we could take a stance too, but that's not really our style, is it, so what with the mayor and Morosity who've clammed up, Albania is alone in her corner, but she still manages to retort:

"Mr. Leaven was seen in the church square. Ten minutes later he was no longer there and the window pane was shattered. I'm simply doing the math. And by the way, what were you doing there, Mr. Leaven?"

"I was out for a walk! Goodness, if I can't set a foot outside without being accused of vandalism, I'd rather close up shop!"

"Well said!"

Old Latvia has the bit between her teeth tonight, and from what we can tell, Albania Meaney doesn't appear to have convinced anyone, in any case certainly not us, what a ridiculous idea, even Father Wavery seems to understand it's beyond a joke, and says in an impassive tone:

"Now, now. We won't get to the bottom of this with insults, my dear brethren. Let's leave it at that for tonight, shall we? Our poor church has enough on its plate at the moment..."

Father Wavery could surely confirm that if the church is still standing today, it's no thanks to the generosity of the Meaneys, as Albania purported, but just as we stand to go up to the sacristy, she jumps in with the last word:

"He's awfully angry, Mr. Leaven, for someone who only last week accused Sybille of stealing..."

Her sister Morosity must have told her the whole saga. What a couple of gossipmongers, those two are! We go upstairs while Giorgio Cantarini waits with an air of despair for his *e basta*, but no one is in the mood for Italianisms tonight.

4

AS ALWAYS, *we* wait impatiently, with bated breath, for the Professor to arrive. He's late, our gift from the heavens! He knows how to play hard to get, and we know how to bide our time. The woman beside us, visibly even more anxious than us, plumps her hair and sniffs loudly.

Ah, at last! There he is, glorious, his scalp glowing beneath the single lightbulb in our lair.

"Good evening, my children."

The woman beside us claps wildly; she's a real devotee, that one! It's the same woman the Professor took aside at the end of last week's meeting. With her woollen clothes and ample girth, she reminds us of a well-fed goose.

"Thank you all, and good evening. And a special thanks to this member, yes, to this valiant warrior who, despite her ailing health, stood up to that dreadful baker on Monday. She symbolizes a true ideal, and each and every one of you would do well to follow her lead."

He points to the portly woman sitting beside us, who blushes, hides her face in her hands, and generally makes a big ado about nothing. We cheer half-heartedly, one eyebrow raised. Jealous, who us? Never!

"But enough of this sweetness, my little bees. The attempt failed, and the baker still reigns supreme over those imbeciles. We must undermine his authority without delay. Without delay!"

We take comfort in the plump goose's newly disheartened demeanour. Dear lady, it's not enough to fall into the Professor's good graces; you have to stay there. But there we go getting sidetracked again, ah, our master has more words of wisdom to share with us:

"Damned baker—accusing people right, left, and centre—and the florist who seems to be siding with him, indeed, my little lambs, we have our work cut out for us."

He pats the pocket of his jacket, his chest rising and falling at an alarming rate, he gets so worked up sometimes!

Suddenly there's a noise. From upstairs. Someone just slammed the door to the church. Someone is now inside the church. Someone is walking in the church!

The Professor's eyes widen, his hands skitter nervously across his skull, his eyes quickly scan the hall and he arrives at the sad conclusion: there's no one missing. Catastrophe. He motions us to be silent. We don't say a word.

And we listen, shoulders hunched, to the slow footsteps making their way across the nave, the sound of heels striking the wooden floor and echoing down the sacristy stairwell.

How terrifying, we haven't been this afraid since the Professor choked on his saliva in the middle of a meeting last year.

The intruder approaches the altar and stops. Then turns back towards the central aisle and reconsiders. We tremble like leaves. The Professor too seems to be gripped by a panic we wouldn't have thought possible of him. He takes his gun out of his jacket pocket. The poor fat lady beside us can't contain herself any longer and whispers:

"Didn't anyone lock the door?"

The Professor glowers at her. What poor judgment; this is not the moment to be asking stupid questions. The intruder now seems to be walking up and down each row of pews looking for something. An eternity goes by as we hear the steps zigzag from one side to the other; it's torture for the woman beside us, who's clapped both hands across her mouth, no doubt terrified she'll let out one of her legendary squeals of anguish.

The intruder heads back across the nave toward the main door and we let out a sigh of relief. The Professor even lowers his gun and pockets it.

Exactly at this crucial moment, one of our members—oblivious, stupid, or perhaps simply feeling the effects of a cold—coughs. A dry, prickly cough that ricochets off the stone walls of the basement and echoes straight up the stairs, we're quite sure! Enraged, the Professor takes his gun out of his pocket again and levels it at the guilty member, down whose cheek rolls a single, silent tear of despair. And, of course, the footsteps in the church start up again, heading back to the altar, approaching the sacristy, and coming down the stairs!

It feels exactly like one of those movies where the sinister shadow of the predator creeps along a castle's bleak stone walls; the click-clack of heels on the wooden steps is unbearable, and the lady in the next chair looks like she's about to faint any second.

His breathing rapid, his face crimson, the Professor turns his gun away and points it toward the staircase.

After an interminable moment, there appears a pair of garish heels, bare legs, then a polka dot dress and an impeccable hairdo. The woman's eyebrows shoot up when she sees us, and she scans the room.

"Good evening, I... I'm looking for my eldest son, I thought I saw him go into the church... My Samuel, he likes to hide in here sometimes. But, what are you all doing here? And you, up there in the front, I know you, what are you doing here, Mr.—"

Alas, she doesn't have time to say our Professor's name; just as she points a finger at him, he pulls the trigger.

We see our life flash before our eyes. Our most cherished moments with our dear Professor. The time he allowed us to hold his coat. The years of happiness and innocence, when our only care in the world was what we would wear to the next meeting.

We open our eyes again. The Professor really did shoot her. Right between the eyes.

The intruder collapses and the fat lady beside us shatters the silence with the squeal of a stuck pig.

"Look what she made me do! Did you see what she made me do, that nosy woman! She had no business coming here to bother us... Now look what she made me do! Go home now, everyone leave and go on home. By the back door if you will, let's try... She had no business coming here tonight, that woman..."

And we file out of the hall, stepping gingerly over the woman's body as we go.

5

THIS WEEK'S MONDAY MEETING has a different feel about it, probably because yesterday was the funeral of Lisa Campbell, the hairdresser, who was killed by a huntsman's stray bullet deep in the woods, where one of her sons stumbled upon her body by accident—how dreadful!—now the child, who was already a little off his rocker, constantly clutches his head and screams. The mayor said a few words at the funeral ceremony, mind you in his case, since one word can stretch into six, a few was more than enough. We're all still in shock. No one has come forward to claim responsibility for the stray bullet, which raises the possibility of murder, but really, who would kill a hairdresser, aside perhaps from a neighbour annoyed with her for letting her children run wild until the wee hours, or a customer whose haircut she botched, but that could be just about anyone, and in any case, a murderer in our midst, what a ridiculous idea, and here goes the baker addressing the gathering:

"Mister Mayor, I believe I'm speaking on behalf of everyone when I ask you to provide us with more details about the death of Mrs. Campbell."

The mayor wishes he were miles away, you can tell by the way the corners of his mouth curl down, but he stands up, because that's what we all expect of him, now let's see what he has to say:

"D-d-dear c-c-constituents, you are all aware of the t-t-tragic circumstances surrounding the death of Li-li-lisa C-c-campbell, I d-d-d-don't have to re-re-re-mind you."

We think the mayor should really learn to get to the crux of the matter instead of telling us what we already know, but maybe it's just sadness and idleness making us talk that way.

"Li-li-lisa C-c-campbell was indeed sh-sho-shot dead by a stray b-b-b-bullet, our friend D-d-d-doctor Harmer has c-c-c-confirmed it."

Doctor Harmer can confirm whatever he likes; he must be pushing eighty by now, with his wrinkled skin and his judgment failing as fast as his eyesight, we really need a new doctor in the village, but who on earth would want such a position? His so-called confirmation leaves us skeptical, but the mayor hasn't finished:

"I'm afraid m-m-my s-s-sister-in-law, Al-Albania, has t-t-taken a t-t-t-urn for the worse this w-w-w-week..."

Apparently the murder of Lisa Campbell has upset Albania Meaney more than the rest of us, even though those two were like cat and dog ever since Albania decided to do her own hair, and yet she's been having a complete breakdown over the past three days, a real drama queen, that one, as we've said before. And if the mayor thinks anyone in their right mind is going to send her flowers and a get-well card, he's got another think coming! His comments are met with sullen silence, and he gets the message and quickly turns back to the problem at hand:

"The huntsman has y-y-yet to identify him-self, b-b-b-but it's only a matter of t-t-t-time. Isn't that so?"

We try to share his optimism, but the baker jumps to his feet in a flash:

"What about Sybille?"

We stifle a gasp, and the mayor replies:

"Wh-wh-what about Sybille?"

"Hasn't it occurred to you that *she* could be the unknown huntsman?"

Two accusations in the space of three weeks—that's a good average for a baker. We know the man's got personality to spare, but now he's outdone the mayor, the priest, the doctor, and even Albania. Note to selves: consider the baker as possible candidate in next municipal election. The mayor's face drops:

"M-m-mister Leaven, haven't I w-w-w-warned everyone about being too quick to make ac-ac-accusations? My re-re-recommendation still stands this week."

The baker frowns, he doesn't like being contradicted, before he was elected mayor, Roger Gross would never have dared stand up to him, but his position of power has obviously given him the confidence to confront the baker, who turns red and huffs:

"All I'm saying is this: Two weeks ago there's a robbery, last week a broken window, this week a murder. What's it going to be next week? A rape? Worse: *genocide*?"

We swallow nervously, genocide, what an awful word. What could it mean? It's so hot in here, and there goes Angelina White putting another log in the stove, what is she thinking? Look at her adjusting her woolen shawl, that old spinster, but the baker has a point: over the past three weeks our world has been turned upside down; whereas before, we had to pray for some miserable scandal to spice up life in the village, now everything is happening too fast. Maybe we should have ferreted out a new police chief when the previous one died of old age three years ago, but then again, who would want to come live here, in the middle of nowhere? We've been negligent all the same. All this brouhaha is making us dizzy, let's try to breathe calmly, ah look, there are the young newlyweds Albert Miller and Blanche Bedford standing up to say something, so far as we know it's the first time they've spoken as Mr. and Mrs. Miller, so it's worth listening to what they have to say:

"We have something to say."

Ah, young people, what do they know, but we forgive them because it's their first time, still, we have to laugh as they explain that they've got something to say, well of course they've got something to say; it's obvious, isn't it? Those more learned than us would call it a pleonasm, but even so, we smile tenderly as Albert explains:

"Sybille cannot be the unknown huntsman."

He cuts a fine figure, young Albert, with his long straight nose and broad shoulders, we can see why Blanche, who has a certain style about her too—all Helga and blonde braids—took a liking to him, but wait, we're getting distracted here. What did he just say?

"I said Sybille is not the unknown huntsman."

Well now! Leaven and Albania may be quick to accuse, but as far as the miller is concerned, Ruth is whiter than his whitest flour, yet does he have any proof? What nerve to contradict the baker! It's enough to earn you nails in your bread, just ask Dr. Harmer, who got exactly that a few years ago, luckily he's a doctor and was able to treat himself, because you can imagine that eating a load of nails full of tetanus for breakfast could seriously upset one's digestion. Ah haa! There goes the baker, he's not going to take that sitting down:

"Ahh, so Sybille is not the unknown huntsman, you say? Then who is, *my children*?"

His expression is as mean-spirited as can be. That's it—the Millers' bread will be stuffed full of rusty screws tomorrow morning, we're sure of it, and now Blanche picks up where Albert left off:

"Baker Leaven, of course we don't know who it is, or we would have gone straight away to the powers that be, as you can well imagine."

The baker's eyebrows arch, as do ours, she's feisty, young Mrs. Miller, and articulate too, rather unusual for a woman her age these days. She goes on:

"What we *do* know—because we saw it with our own eyes—is that Sybille was not in the woods at Mrs. Campbell's presumed time of death."

Then she sits back down and blushes abruptly. That's all well and good, but why should we take her at her word, how does she know that, and where was Sybille if she wasn't in the forest because, between you and us, the only time of the year Sybille isn't in the woods is on her birthday, at least we assume it's her birthday because she parades through the village all decked out in her fanciest get-up like it's carnival day, putting on airs and singing in her own tongue, it's a natural catastrophe that occurs every September, but that's beside the point, let's hear what Albert Miller has to say:

"That's right. That day Sybille was at the mill up on the hill."

We're stunned by the revelation. Sybille at the mill? Whatever for? We instantly make a connection: perhaps she decided that, instead of snitching the baker's loaves, she'd go straight to the source and swipe the flour instead, which would automatically incriminate her for robbery, a crime we've suspected her of all along, let's see what more young Albert can tell us, he's begun to blush, maybe it's his blood pressure:

"You see, that day after work, I stayed on at the mill for a while, and Blanche came to join me there."

Now, why on earth would he have stayed after work, everyone's free to go home at the end of their work day, that's the rule, but the baker jumps in and puts the question to him before we have a chance to ask, as we said earlier, he's a real big mouth, that one, and Albert replies:

"We stayed at the mill because we felt like it, that's all. The reason why doesn't matter. Anyway, while we were lying near the grindstones, we heard a noise, and when we stood up and looked out the window, we saw Sybille prowling around the mill. I don't know what she was doing there, but it was most definitely her, and I can tell you it was exactly eight o'clock—the time Dr. Harmer says Mrs. Campbell was killed—because I heard the church bells chiming in the distance."

Interesting! Now, Sybille has a solid alibi, she has Albert and Blanche to thank for that if ever she bumps into them at the mill or elsewhere, they've just saved her skin, but that's just gone and thrown a wrench in the works—who could have pulled the trigger if it wasn't Sybille, and did the Miller boy say they were *lying* near the grindstones, but before we can take that thought any further, the baker stands up again:

"Mr. Mayor, Father Wavery, Dr. Harmer, with all the respect I owe these children, I must question the credibility of their testimony. Did they really see Sybille? At eight o'clock, the sun is setting and it's hard to see clearly. Perhaps it was someone else they saw? And then there's the question of what the young couple were doing *lying* in the flour?"

He doesn't miss a beat, our baker, but we must admit that we too are curious as to what the two young lovers could have been up to, lying together at a mill, it must be another of their tall tales, we can't make head nor tail of it, and now it's a very scarlet Blanche who replies:

"*Primo*, what we were doing is nobody's business but ours. *Secundo*, yes, it was definitely Sybille, we recognized her hair. *Tertio*, we are not children, and *quarto*, don't bother baking any bread for us tomorrow, Mr. Leaven; we'll be finding ourselves another baker, thank you very much."

What a joker, that girl, *we'll be finding another baker*! Good luck, what with Leaven and his monopoly on dough for miles around, but one man who must be pleased is Giorgio Cantarini with all those Italian words, they always were close, those two, and where is Cantarini anyway? We can't see him anywhere, what's the point of allowing him his *e basta* if he's not even there to hear it, in any case, the testimony of the young ones is all of a sudden more believable, they say they recognized Sybille by her hair, and that is altogether probable, you've really got to see that woman's hair to understand, it's impossible to describe, suffice to say it's something of an ecological disaster, oh look, there goes Father Wavery—again!—eager to have his say:

"That's enough for today. We won't learn the huntsman's identity this evening, that much is clear. Now it's time to go on home and pray, pray that no further tragedy befalls our village, pray for the soul of our friend Lisa Campbell."

There he goes again, cutting short the meeting, not that we really mind, after all we have to admit that over the past two weeks our Monday meetings have been something of a roller coaster ride. Let's go home to bed, it's getting late, Old Man Harmer has already been asleep on his chair for a good half-hour, he's ready for retirement, that one.

6

IT'S FRIDAY, *we*'re having fun. We watch each other out of the corner of our eye, we smile at each other, our hearts are so very light. That's because at their Monday meeting, they practically exonerated Sybille. All thanks to the testimony of two of our members. We slept better this week, and we're sure the Professor did too. He's keeping us waiting, as is his wont, we keep an eye on the rostrum in case he appears out of nowhere by some sleight of hand. Perhaps our two courageous colleagues will be awarded a medal of honour. We tap our feet and smile.

At last! The Professor appears. We stand and greet him with thunderous applause. The two young heroes blush with pride. Our eyes turn to our master.

His lips are trembling, his eyes bloodshot. He points his divine finger at the couple in question:

"You!"

Yes, them! Tears well in our eyes; we're writing a page of History, what a wonderful and unique opportunity. The Professor repeats:

"You! *You!*"

He doesn't look as happy as we do, but we continue to cheer even louder. Our enthusiasm is bound to win him over. Goodness, how presumptuous of us! Influence the Professor? Us? The idea delights us, we even feel a little bashful; our cheeks flush as we continue to clap.

"Silence!"

We fall silent. Such an enigmatic Professor we have, so unpredictable! Surely the sign of a genius.

"Miserable little swine!" he whispers.

He's suddenly sweating profusely. His face turns purple. Who is he talking to? Who will have the honour of an affectionate nickname? The Professor says it again, this time a little louder:

"Miserable little swine!"

Now it's clear. He's pointing straight at our two brave members, the very same two who managed to get Sybille off the hook.

"Who asked you to testify on Sybille's behalf?"

The young newlyweds bite their lips in pale silence. Even from our viewpoint we can see they're gripping each other's hands so tightly their fingernails have gone white. The woman clears her throat and speaks up:

"Professor, no one asked us to. We simply thought that Sybille and all our fellow members would be relieved to have us shoulder part of the burden."

She projects her words in a powerful, juvenile tone; we raise our eyebrows. It's an impressive performance before a man of the Professor's stature. But it takes more than that, much more, to disarm our master. A smile plays on his lips. What has he got up his sleeve for us now?

"Look at them. So young. So blond. So oblivious."

He scans the room.

"Don't do it again. Ever. There's only one person here who calls the shots."

Oh, how we long for him to ask us who that person is; we know the answer. We twitch with anticipation, but the question never comes, and the Professor spits:

"And that's *me!*"

Oh! Oh.

"Off with you now. I've seen enough of you all. Off to bed! To bed!"

We leave the room, vaguely disappointed.

7

WHAT A WONDERFUL WEEK IT'S BEEN, in truth a week as normal as can be, but the mere fact there has been no drama other than Amelia Gross having her wisdom teeth removed is enough to lift our spirits, brighten our mood, soothe our nerves. If Sybille had attended the Monday meeting she would surely have proclaimed that the curse had been broken—her and her druidess talk—and for once we would have let her ramble on because it really wouldn't bother us, but where on earth is Mr. Gross? The mayor's never late for anything, that's his most notable quality, we bet Mrs. Latvia the florist knows, after all she knows everything, right down to the late-night habits of the baker, let's ask her and see what gossip she'll serve us up this time:

"Mayor Gross? What, am I the only one with eyes and ears in this village?"

Mrs. Latvia wraps everything about herself in euphemism and overblows everything about everyone else, they say it's typical of pathological liars and histrionic personalities, but what do we know; we're only repeating what we once over-heard Dr. Harmer telling the late Lisa Campbell, and now it's the baker who jumps in:

"With all due respect, Mrs. Latvia, every one of us here has eyes and ears, only most of us know well enough to leave them at home where they belong."

There go the florist's glasses fogging up, such a sensitive woman, or maybe she's faking it, it's hard to tell from where we're sitting. The baker had best retract his comments, how's he going to get himself out of this one? And now Mrs. Latvia takes out a ridiculous pink handkerchief and sniffles:

"I'm only trying to help. If you don't want answers, don't ask questions. I'm at my wits' end here, looking after three babies *on my own* at my age and with no pension. It's no picnic, I can tell you."

We have to give her that. Since last week she's had to take the Campbell kids under her wing, and three ill-bred orphans under the same roof as an elderly florist, well, you can imagine the scene—more tragedy than comedy, if you ask us, what with the eldest who spends his days clutching his head and screaming ever since he stumbled across the bloody corpse of his mother—it's understandable—just think of Mrs. Latvia with two little ones missing their mother and a third who cries night and day, if on top of all that she has to sell her bouquets to make ends meet and endure the baker's insults too, well, what is this world coming to?

She continues:

"She had to go and put me in her will, that Lisa Campbell. She couldn't just have left her kids to a young one like Blanche Bedford or to a wealthy spinster like Angelina White, no, of course not! She had to go and burden poor Latvia. For some there's no rest until they're six feet under, and I'm sure that will be my fate too. I'm warning you, one day you'll find me dead as a doornail among my French lilies if I keep up this pace. I'm not twenty anymore, you know!"

Even the baker looks touched. With his jowly cheeks and his jaw unclenched, he looks almost friendly. We could swear we saw a tear of compassion roll down his cheek just now, but surely it's just a figment of our imagination. Perhaps Mrs. Latvia is ready to answer us, now that she's unburdened herself in public, so we try again. She blows her nose into her hankie and stands up:

"The mayor is with Amelia, as a matter of fact. She has taken a turn for the worse, and he wanted to be by her side."

Goodness, we had no idea Amelia wasn't doing well. We were under the impression that getting one's wisdom teeth removed was a minor operation, we shift our gaze as one toward the elderly doctor because, of course, we don't have a dentist in the village, and the doctor has always insisted he can do the job of both dentist and GP, but with eighty years under his belt, we have to wonder what's left of the man's memory, even if he *is* a doctor.

The mayor might have realized that an ounce of prevention is worth a pound of cure and sent his daughter to town to have her teeth out, where you'd think there are dental surgeons, but he didn't. Mind you, he's been a firm devotee of Harmer since the doctor saved Morosity Gross's life during the difficult birth of their daughter

Amelia, speaking of the doctor, he gets up to speak:

"Allow me to enlighten you."

Dr. Harmer's voice is more tremulous than ever, and his hands are just as shaky, which is getting to be a real challenge for the apothecary, who has to decipher the doctor's prescriptions, but never mind that, let's listen to the old man:

"You see, removing a patient's wisdom teeth is a minor operation. In fact, it's very straightforward."

If it's so straightforward, why is he telling us, it's making us anxious, this whole situation with Amelia, especially since we thought the curse had been broken at last, but the old doctor hasn't finished:

"However, as I was operating on Amelia, I noted that the child—the adolescent, I should say—appeared to have a swollen throat. And being a conscientious doctor, I decided to kill two birds with one stone, you see."

We do *not* see at all, should we say as much, at the risk of looking like idiots in the eyes of a man of science, but the baker doesn't share our fear:

"We see nothing whatsoever, Dr. Harmer. Nothing in the slightest."

"Well it's quite simple. I wanted to examine her throat more closely but I forgot about the tool I was holding—a pair of pliers—and I uhh..."

And he uhh he uhh he uhhh what? That's what you call the revenge of the senile doctor, all this suspense surrounding the Gross girl, is he going to tell us what happened or not?

"As you can imagine, I was startled when I realized the poor child had a pair of extraction pliers stuck nearly as far back as her tonsils, and I must say, I still can't believe she didn't feel a thing."

We can only imagine the scene, a shiver of disgust runs down our spine—pliers stuck in the girl's gullet and the doctor's putrid breath in her face to boot, no wonder Amelia's condition took a turn for the worse, but the old man has more to add:

"And I was so startled I accidentally scraped the inside of her mouth, her throat, with my pliers. As you can imagine, it sent me into a panic, and I began to shake and shake, and she began to bleed and bleed and cry. Oh, this profession is too much for an old man like me!"

We shudder at the thought. It's like something out of a horror movie, the doctor torturing his helpless patient as she lies, defenceless, on the old sadist's chair and when, to make matters worse, the victim is a rosebud of a girl like Amelia Gross, the tragedy is threefold, but what has become of the poor thing, Harmer is about to tell us:

"Amelia is fighting an infection caused by the cuts inflicted by my pliers. I have every hope that under my care, and that of Mr. Meaney, she will be back on her feet within a month. I cannot hide the fact that she is suffering terribly. But I am certain that the support of her parents—and your prayers—are of great comfort to her."

Ah! Our prayers. We will pray for her, starting tomorrow evening, we promise, poor Amelia, poor Mayor Gross, and poor Morosity, as if the girl hadn't suffered enough in her lifetime with the whole pen-pinching story, now she's battling a serious infection, this from a girl who has always claimed to anyone who'll listen that she won't live a day past fourteen, those of a more pessimistic nature may now be inclined to believe her. The parish hall suddenly falls silent, even the baker crosses himself and prays, as a matter of form, and the doctor, who's looking more confident now that he realizes we aren't going to hold his incompetence against him, takes advantage of the lull to announce:

"On that note, go on back home. And send your positive thoughts to the Gross family."

We will, they can count on us, in fact we'll ask Mrs. Latvia to take them a gigantic bouquet, that'll take her mind off things, the poor old crone is so lonely and bored.

8

WE'RE IN FOR A PLEASANT SURPRISE when we arrive at the parish hall today. The Professor is already there, pacing up and down, clearing his throat and patting his pant pocket. We take our seats in silence; when our master is preoccupied, it's best to keep quiet. He turns to look at us, his eyes puffy:

"Dear colleagues, welcome."

That's a good sign. He carries on:

"This has been a week of insomnia for me. The first in years."

We wince in sympathy. We know only too well: when the Professor doesn't sleep well, a catastrophe is surely imminent. The man is so much more learned than us in the ways of the world. He continues, his voice expressionless:

"Only last week I blamed my two miserable little swine..."

We glance over at the young newlyweds, who are clearly moved at being the focus of attention all over again.

"...and yet this week, I made a mistake. Perhaps the biggest mistake of my life."

Our stomach churns, our head spins. How could the Professor be wrong? It's enough to make us question the very foundations of our existence. We hazard a comment:

"Professor, you're too hard on yourself."

He pulls his revolver out of his pocket and points it at us, his hand trembling for the first time:

"Keep quiet. Keep quiet. Keep quiet. Unless you want to fall by example like that other one. The hairdresser. Keep quiet."

So we keep quiet. To die by example at our mentor's hand would give us great joy, but to do so would mean going against the Professor's wishes, a repulsive notion. He lowers his gun and speaks again:

"The daughter of one of our members is suffering terribly as we speak. I'm sure you know who I am talking about."

Alas, we do! That's all everyone's been talking about this week, the poor girl with the infected mouth, rumour has it that her gums have rotted so fast all her teeth have dropped out.

"You probably think—wrongly—the person responsible for this tragedy is our colleague the doctor."

Indeed, that's exactly what we think, they say he completely lacerated her mouth with his rusty pliers. The Professor shouts:

"Well, think again! Of course our friend the GP injured the girl, but..."

Our throat is suddenly dry.

"... but he did so at my request. That's right, at my specific request. On my orders."

Our master bursts into violent sobs. We look at each other in amazement. A large teardrop hangs off the end of the Professor's nose, and his gold-rimmed glasses are all askew. We feel like comforting him, singing him a lullaby, but it wouldn't be right. We wait until he composes himself. He continues speaking, his voice hoarse:

"I thought a little incident would divert attention from the whole unknown huntsman affair. I knew the girl was going to have her wisdom teeth out. I told the doctor to botch the operation—just a little—to distract those imbeciles."

Our colleague the doctor stands:

"Only I botched it *completely*. You understand, what with the stress, my age..."

His eyes swim with tears. We're on the verge of bawling in unison, but our master hasn't finished:

"And now she is suffering. In agony. And it's my fault."

Fortunately the stricken girl's father is absent tonight. What a tragedy for the family.

"And now we must pray. Pray that everything works out, that the girl survives. Oh!"

Once again, tears spring from his eyes. This time, we can't hold back. We join him in his anguish, we give in to an outpouring of emotion. The hall fills with haunting wails. If the girl had been there, what a comfort it would have been for her, even if she were to die, at least she would know how we were moved by her misfortune. We look at each other, tears in our eyes, and think what a wonderful family we are. The Professor takes the gun out of his pocket again:

"But this week, no mistakes. No slip-ups. We keep calm. Understood, you idiots?"

Ahh, that's our beloved mentor speaking, such a genius. Not afraid to plunge headfirst into his emotions, though never for too long, then—in a flash!—he's back. He pulls himself together and leads us to reason. Such a great man. Now we're sobbing in admiration. We file out of the basement, handkerchiefs in hand, praying for... what was it again? Yes, praying that the Professor never leaves our side.

9

A MONSTROUS WEEK, that's the only way to describe it—monstrous—and don't think for a minute we're exaggerating! You only have to ask Morosity Gross, who's been by Amelia's bedside day and night for the past eight days without sleeping a wink. According to Mrs. Latvia, she's so exhausted she looks worse than her daughter, and God knows the child is in terrible shape, what with the infection of her entire oral cavity, gums molars canines tongue included. Angelina White says her breath is so fetid that even Sybille was unable to stifle a cry of disgust when she passed beneath the bedroom window yesterday, and if there's anyone here who has a stomach for repugnant odours, it's Sybille. Aside from the case of the girl who's rotting from the inside of her mouth, Mrs. Latvia asked the council tonight to be relieved of the Campbell children:

"It's simply not right to ask an elderly florist like me to run around after three youngsters all day long, especially when there's one who's always dreaming about death."

It's true, the eldest is officially suicidal, Dr. Harmer confirmed it after a thorough psychological examination; apparently he must never be left alone with knives, scissors, a gun, or a bottle of pills, and when you consider that Mrs. Latvia's shop is full of secateurs and her night table laden with tablets to fight off boredom, the child must indeed be causing her no end of worry. Except, if Mrs. Latvia gets rid of the kids, who's going to take them? After all, Lisa Campbell specifically named the florist as a worthy adoptive mother to her litter, can the wishes of the deceased really be ignored so easily? The baker gets to his feet—in the mayor's absence, he's clearly taking his ease—and proclaims:

"Mrs. Latvia is right. Look at her. Look at her! She must have aged ten years in two weeks."

We all take a good look at her. It's true her crow's feet are a little more pronounced than before, but that's normal at her age. We've always thought of her not just as the florist, but as the founder of the village. It's as if she's been around forever, knows every stone and board in every house, has seen and heard it all, but that's the stuff of legends, and if you ask her, she'll surely tell you she's no older than any of the others, barely older than Albania, and certainly not as old as that witch Sybille. But if you ask us, she must be pushing a hundred and two.

"I'm sixty-six years old and I can't foresee the day I'll be allowed to rest. It's not as if she left her young ones to a well-off family like the Grosses. She left me peanuts to look after those children. Mere *peanuts*, I'm telling you!"

Only sixty-six, poor old Mrs. Latvia, we never would have believed it. She pulls out her embroidered hankie, here come the tears:

"It's African violets I sell, you know, not diamonds! And now if I have to scrounge for money to make the stews and jelly doughnuts they're so fond of, well, my Dutch tulips will end up straight in the garbage. Farewell, my English roses!"

The old woman manages to extract a sigh of pity from us, and even a droplet from the corner of our eye. Hah, she has a real knack for melodrama or is it expressionism, whatever, we're not too up on the world of cinema, what we mean is that she has a knack for bringing a tear to the eye, even when she's at the end of her tether. Blanche Bedford stands up—she's getting chattier by the minute, that one, as bold as a baker, we won't put up with it for long, but for now we let it pass—and puts on her best young Audrey Hepburn voice:

"If Mrs. Latvia no longer wishes to shoulder the heavy burden of these children... I am willing to take over. That is an official offer."

The florist recovers her composure and crumples her perfumed handkerchief:

"Blanche Bedford celebrated her first communion barely six years ago, I remember because I was the one who provided the flowers to decorate the church!"

Flustered, she points at the young woman:

"Far too young, my girl. You are far too young and inexperienced for that. It's an ordeal! One of the modern scourges sent by the Creator to test old Latvia, nothing less. I warn you, my dear: the eldest spends his days sleeping or spitting at his brothers whenever they come near. And the brothers aren't much better: The teacher says they barely know how to count on their fingers. At their age!"

The young bride stamps her foot, a surprising gesture for one who prides herself on her maturity, and yet... Such a childish reflex! She replies:

"Mrs. Latvia, you must make up your mind. Look at you—all teary-eyed and on edge, at an age when you should be making your funeral arrangements. Isn't it time you enjoyed life a bit? While Albert and I have our whole lives ahead of us. And in any case, do you see anyone else stepping up to volunteer?"

We scan the room, not a single hand is raised, not like during our votes, not even Angelina White, the wealthy—and then some!—old spinster, or Leaven the baker, who's always saying he'd make an excellent father if only a woman would give him the chance. Then there's old Giorgio Cantarini who raises his finger, but no one takes him seriously, not since the day the late Lisa Campbell swore he used to peek under her skirt while she swept up hair clippings, we don't consider him an appropriate candidate for raising three children. And anyway, with his meagre war widower's pension, all he can afford to eat is beans in tomato sauce, when we know full well the little ones are used to chicken pie and sticky buns!

The baker, who we notice has been shifting restlessly on his chair for the past few minutes, decides to take charge of the meeting:

"That's enough! Have we forgotten our manners, our procedures? This type of situation must be decided by a show of hands. All those who think young Blanche Bedford should take the Campbell children, raise your hands nice and high!"

Ah, spoken with the authority of our loaf-maker, and we raise our hand straight up, as high as it will go so we can move on to the next thing other than feeling sorry for Mrs. Latvia, and looking around the room, we notice that everyone, except for that old romantic Cantarini, and obedient Angelina White, is doing the same, which brings a smile to the face of the baker, who booms:

"*E basta!*"

Cantarini squirms with delight, he looks like he's about to launch into a few verses of Dante in a burst of nostalgia, but our dear Latvia has other plans, and she leaps up like a jack-in-a-box:

"I call on the priest to decide!"

The priest, what a ridiculous idea, we chuckle to ourselves, even Father Wavery is wearing a rather disbelieving grin, and then, as usual, Blanche adopts the schoolmarmish tone that earned her mother a reputation back in the day when she used to teach painting to the old folks:

"This is not simply up to you, Mrs. Latvia. Where the safety of the children is a concern— and I believe it may well be—we cannot take any risks."

The florist straightens up in her chair and lifts her nose towards the heavens, appropriately enough, given the premises:

"Safety, safety! Those children are better off with me and my chrysanthemums than with Lisa Campbell and her shenanigans!"

Now, we have to admit we're not quite following: what exactly is she talking about? While the late Lisa Campbell may have allowed her children to play in the street a little too often, she nevertheless struck us as a worthy mother, although, *worthy* is no doubt too strong a word in her case, but at the very least, she never lost any of her young ones in the woods, and knowing their nature, that's an achievement that surely deserves a trophy. The baker immediately demands an explanation:

"What are these accusations against the deceased, Mrs. Latvia? That's not like you."

Look who's talking, the man who's been knocking Sybille at every chance he gets for the past three weeks, mind you it's not as though Sybille is actually dead, although who really knows, maybe she's just some sort of creature of witchcraft risen from her ashes. The old florist frowns:

"Oh, I know what I know!"

She's playing with our nerves again, that sly woman, and there she goes with a second tragic waving of the hankie, dabbing at her eyes, and now all it takes is Cantarini rubbing her back—speaking of which, they'd make a fine pair, those two, it would calm them down and would suit us just fine too—to get her started again:

"Ahh, now I have your attention! No one listens to the old lady until she starts dishing out the gossip. Well if that's how it's going to be... Let me tell you what I overhead one day while I was waiting in Lisa Campbell's hair salon."

All ears perk up, especially Dr. Harmer's, who's hard of hearing, and the florist continues:

"I was sitting comfortably in the waiting room of Lisa Campbell's salon and I could hear Lisa finishing up Angelina White's hair. It was December 18 of last year; I remember because it was snowing hard, and I really hoped she would finish my hair in time so I wouldn't get lost in the storm on my way home.

"Then the phone rang. I was a bit angry, because I was afraid the call would set me back even later. From where I was sitting, in the corner of the waiting room, I could hear everything that went on at the counter, so when Lisa Campbell left Angelina to answer the phone, I was able to follow the entire conversation with no trouble, and, more importantly, without being seen, and let me tell you, what I heard took my mind off the storm completely.

"Now, get this: she was talking to a man—she called him by his name 'James' several times—and she appeared to know him well. And when I say 'well' I mean they weren't chatting about the weather or about Sybille, if you get my drift.

"I knew, just as well as you, that Bertrand Campbell had skipped out the year before, leaving poor Lisa with his young ones. But I also knew, thanks to Sybille, that Bertrand Campbell's brother is named—wait for it !—*James*.

"So, when Lisa Campbell hung up, and it must have been a good fifteen minutes later—because Angelina White's half-dried locks certainly weren't going to stop her from talking to her James—I figured I was going to have to keep waiting, so I might as well make the most of the situation.

"I waited until she'd gone back to Angelina in the other room before going and sitting behind the counter. Finding her address book was child's play; she'd left it right beside the telephone. I remember I stopped at the page my own number was on and saw that the idiot—God save her soul—had forgotten to change my address when I moved. I corrected it myself in red pen, out of principle and to teach her a lesson, even if she never called me except when her little monsters were causing her grief, never just to see how I was doing.

"After that, I quickly flipped back to the C page to see if James's number was there. And that's when things got complicated."

Mrs. Latvia pauses a moment and clasps her hands together, as if in silent prayer to a God watching over us, just above. What she's praying for we haven't the faintest idea, but the baker immediately asks her if she will, pray tell, continue her story:

"As I was saying, I was going through the Cs to prove that the mysterious caller was none other than James Campbell, Lisa's brother-in-

80

law. And just as I was about to find out, the salon door suddenly opened. Angelina and Lisa were chatting away in the other room, and with the noise of the hair dryer, they didn't hear the bell ring as the door opened.

"I looked up, and who should I see, staring at me with an accusing look? Who? Blanche Bedford!"

We all turn as one to look at young Blanche, she who prides herself on never being part of the problem; only the solution. Well, that was quite a testimony from Mrs. Latvia, and now Blanche blushes. If you ask us, she knows only too well what the florist is about to reveal:

"There's no point staring at Blanche with your Lobster Thermidor eyes. She is of no importance, so don't lend her any more than she deserves.

"Back then, she wasn't yet wed to Albert Miller, eligible young lady that she was. She came into the salon and asked me what I was doing sitting at Lisa Campbell's desk. I told her I was helping Lisa with her paperwork, that the poor woman had plenty on her hands with her three boys, and that, in any case, it wasn't carnation season yet. She nodded. I could tell she didn't believe me, that she imagined I was rummaging through Lisa Campbell's bills or her receipts for ammonia hair dye, so I had to fill her in.

"I told her briefly about the phone call, the man's name, the coincidence, the gist of it. And then, believe it or not, the dear child offered to help me in my search!

"James Campbell's name didn't appear anywhere in the address book, but that didn't stop Blanche; she left such a mess turning the dresser drawers inside out that I had to follow behind her and put everything back in its place.

"Nothing! There was nothing there—Blanche can vouch for me—except receipts for hair dye and dozens of licorice candy wrappers, all carefully smoothed out and stacked in an old cigar box.

"We were about to give up on the desk and sit back down in the waiting room, because we could hear Angelina White thanking Lisa Campbell and preparing to get up out of the chair, when Blanche spotted a crumpled piece of paper half hidden under the telephone, only one corner peeking out, as if to tease us.

"Blanche was up in a flash and grabbed that paper! My friends, that's what I call luck, because just as we were taking our seats again in the waiting room, Lisa Campbell came to greet us, all smiles and fresh curls, for our respective hair appointments.

"'Ahh, my most senior and junior customers! How touching to see you together, chatting like the best girlfriends in the village.'"

We should clarify here: we stated earlier that Sybille is the oldest woman in the village, but Sybille has never set foot in the Campbell hair salon to have her hair done. As we said, her hair is in a constant state of humanitarian crisis, and could certainly use a good combing to put its internal affairs in order. But what do you expect when you choose to live like a savage, there are no half measures, let's hear what else Mrs. Latvia has to say:

"Lisa Campbell was wearing her figure-flattering, blue woolen dress, I remember because when she saw her in it, Blanche immediately began smoothing and adjusting her own outfit, whether out of jealousy or some hang-up, or simple female vanity, who knows.

"I got up and made sure I beat Blanche to Lisa's chair, after all I was there first, and in any case, who was to say whether young Blanche had actually come to get her hair done and not just to nose around looking for gossip.

"You all knew the late Lisa: she had a voice that carried, sometimes gossip, often lewd remarks, whatever the case, it was a voice that carried. And when a voice like that squawks inches away from your eardrums, it's enough to make you tune out altogether. The whole time she was doing my hair, I didn't hear or see a thing of what was going on in the waiting room, thanks to Lisa Campbell's chatter and the awkward angle of the mirror.

"So imagine my surprise when I went to the counter to pay and saw that Blanche had disappeared without a word! Like a thief in the night, and taking with her the scrap of paper from under the phone! Lisa was no less surprised, but she surmised that Blanche must have worried the storm was picking up and that she'd be stuck at the salon all night. In any case, Lisa Campbell was never one to bother much about such things. As for me, I went out into the storm and since that day I haven't had a chance to talk to Blanche Bedford alone. So, the mystery remains unsolved."

Mrs. Latvia catches her breath and sits down, clearly pleased with herself, her expression calm and serene, as it always is after recounting some juicy anecdote or other or delivering a big bouquet of gladioli. No more than two seconds pass before Angelina White blurts out:

"What about the paper? What did it say? What did it say?"

Coming from such a paragon of modesty and discretion, her reaction is somewhat surprising; no doubt she finds the florist's tale titillating because, for once, she's part of it. Mrs. Latvia throws up her hands:

"I don't know! I never saw that damned piece of paper again! Blanche Bedford kept it."

The entire room turns to face the young woman, who looks offended and keeps her gaze on the floor. The baker, never one to miss an opportunity, addresses her in his most inquisitorial tone:

"Blanche, we are all waiting for an answer."

He's obviously still angry at her for changing bread suppliers, but really, where else is she going to get her loaves now that she's boycotting Leaven? Perhaps she's got Albert Miller eating crackers—a tall order knowing how the young man likes his rolls crusty and warm—anyway, in the meantime, Blanche says nothing, while her husband stares at her in horror. Evidently, she never told him about the stolen paper, but the baker insists:

"All I can say is this: once a thief, always a thief."

We raise our eyebrows. The baker is clearly referring to the breadlifting of which he was a victim, the *Leaven Affair*, as we've fondly dubbed it, he still hasn't fully digested the whole thing, it's left a hard ball in the pit of his stomach, like a lump of unleavened bread. Albert Miller stands up to have his say, a rare occasion indeed since his marriage to the opinionated Blanche:

"Blanche did not steal your bread, Mr. Leaven, the entire council has accepted the fact: it was Sybille, because nobody else would have left a bowl of wild strawberries in return."

"Ahh! But strawberries can be picked, and bowls can be made!"

Now he's pushing it, Leaven! We whistle anxiously, what's going to happen now?

"Mr. Leaven, you are forgetting that the real snoop here is Mrs. Latvia. She's the one who mixed Blanche up in this whole James story. Why couldn't it have been her who stole your bread, too, while casting the blame on Sybille?"

"Because she's a little old lady!"

If there's one thing the florist can't stand, it's being reminded of her venerable age, so out comes the hankie again, and she sniffles and snuffles for a time. Cantarini, who's still beside her rubbing her back, suddenly jumps up and pours forth:

"What if this whole story about James and the telephone had something to do with the unknown huntsman and the death of Lisa Campbell?"

Goodness, what progress old Cantarini has made! Give him another few months and we're willing to bet he'll be fully functional, but for now Father Wavery has chosen this critical moment to raise his hands, his palms towards the heavens:

"My children, we won't get to the bottom of the story this evening. It's obvious the cards of Providence are all mixed up. Let's sleep on this and consider it again with fresh eyes. It's getting late and there's a storm brewing."

There he goes again with his confounded habit of cutting our meetings short! If we had the baker's gumption, we would protest, but instead we lower our head and leave the hall, disbelieving and troubled. What with all that, the baker's irritation, and Father Wavery's orders, Blanche never did tell us what happened to the scrap of paper.

10

THE PROFESSOR APPEARS BEFORE US at the meeting. He's looking perplexed, and *we*'re not sure whether that's a good or bad sign. Who can fathom the expression of a god?

This week, our gathering stretches all the way to the staircase leading up to the sacristy; it seems some of our members who have been absent recently have decided to pick up their good habits again, among them the parents of the ailing girl. The Professor gives us a brief nod and begins:

"My children, this has been another week of surprising revelations. Will it never end? Will we ever return to the peace and quiet of previous years of petty crime?"

That's the burning question that's been haunting us for the past month, and now the Professor is asking us as if we knew the answer, as if we could possibly know better than him—if we had a crystal ball, perhaps, but just like that, on the spot, impossible!

"The woman who agreed to care for the children of the hairdresser who died two weeks ago has abandoned her burden, forcing one of our members—one of our youngest members, in fact—to step in."

It's true, the young woman so devoted to the cause and to the proper education of three future members—what a model of altruism! The very same young woman who provided Sybille with an alibi, clearing her name in the burglary she was accused of. A member with great promise indeed. The Professor clasps his hands together—he looks almost humble—and says:

"There are two things I'd like to do. First, congratulate this member—Yes, you!—the young girl who adopted the orphans."

And she deserves it, the brave child. We clap modestly: the Professor doesn't like it when we praise someone other than him. She lowers her eyes and blushes. He continues:

"But I also want to warn you."

His gaze hardens. He raises his hand in the girl's direction, and we all know from experience that it's not so he can shower her with candy. He points his index finger at her and cautions:

"You did a good thing. ONE good thing. But don't let it go to your head. In here it's the Professor who calls the shots. He's the one who makes the rules and writes the laws. In future, before you go taking any initiative whatsoever, you ask my permission first."

What joy, what good fortune for the young girl! To have the Professor acknowledge her courage must fill her, her parents, her husband with such pride! But still, she'd better mind herself now. If she goes against the Professor's will she could face the same fate as that poor snoop who died accidentally three weeks ago.

After delivering his warning, the Professor gives the floor over to our fellow members whose child is recovering from an infection, though, as they tell us, she doesn't actually appear to be on the mend.

"Our sweet little darling is having a very difficult time of it, Professor, a terrible time. If it gets any worse, she'll have to have her entire head amputated, with all the pus it's oozing. The pain is one thing, but she has to endure the humiliation too. Even Sybille expressed her disgust the other day. And if my daughter is to be held in contempt by someone like Sybille, I'd almost rather see her dead. It's such an ordeal, I assure you!"

It's the mother who has spoken. She doesn't seem to blame our leader and, anyway, the young girl will look back fondly on her ordeal later— she'll probably even be awarded a municipal medal once she's better. The Professor's lips tremble and tears well in his eyes. He looks like he's on the verge of hugging the parents. But he says nothing, and we can tell he's tormented by his decision, by his failure, and so is the doctor. We wish we could share their suffering, ease it, lessen it, but the best we can do is shed a few tears in empathy, and in the face of the Professor's sadness, our faith in life evaporates.

Once he regains his composure, our leader sends us home for a melancholy night. He motions to the courageous young girl and takes her aside. As we leave the hall we hear him ask her:

"That piece of paper the old woman was talking about, what did you do with it?"

11

WE'RE NOT SURE HOW BEST TO DESCRIBE this
past week. Those more educated than us would
no doubt call it Kafkaesque; all we can say is that
it was one of anguish—anguish and politics—
because the baker had half the village sign a
petition to force the young Bedford girl to reveal
the contents of the scrap of paper at tonight's
meeting. We say "half the village" because even
if the baker had wanted to get Sybille to sign it,
she likely wouldn't have—and anyway, we've
never seen any proof that she knows how to read
or write, or that she even has her own opinions—
and if you don't count the children; the priest

and the mayor, who are supposed to remain impartial; Blanche herself; and Albert, who abstained for fear of being subjected to years of matrimonial drought, that makes nearly half, if we've counted right: half of the villagers signed that damned petition—God save our souls!

This evening in the church basement, we're burning with impatience as we wait for Blanche, who's late—it's not like her to be late—but we would have been late too, if we were in her shoes. Latvia the florist holds her head high, scornfully eyeing the baker who clutches, crumpled in his floury hands, the Petition—that's how he refers to his project—Petition with a capital P if you please, it's a wonder he hasn't had it blessed by Father Wavery. Blanche must still be powdering her nose or whatever it is that women do at times like this. Call it the revenge of the young virgin.

At last! We hear footsteps on the stairs, our necks swivel as one, like bolts being unscrewed a turn, and a head pops into the room, a head that doesn't belong to Blanche Bedford.

It's the eldest Campbell boy.

He comes down the stairs, one foot then the other on each step, like a baby, it's obvious with the death of his mother he's regressed at least five years, his big brown curls tumbling over his eyes. Mrs. Latvia shoots out of her chair:

"Samuel! Samuel Campbell, what are you doing here? What did I tell you? That Blanche is too young to take care of such a disturbed child. When I think that I sent her a basket of geraniums to thank her, now I regret it; if I'd known, I'd have sent her a bunch of lily of the valley!"

Mrs. Latvia abhors lily of the valley.

The Campbell boy lowers his head and looks at us like in one of those stories where the child has the soul of an adult and the mind of an assassin in the body of a youth, and even the florist cuts short her complaint, it's enough to give you nightmares, those eyes as dark as the well at the end of St. Andrew's Street.

He walks to the middle of the room, the soles of his muddy boots squeaking on the floor tiles—it must be raining out, it's a good thing we shut the windows before we left.

When he gets to Mrs. Latvia's chair, the Campbell boy grabs his head with both hands.

"You see! That's all he does, clutch his noggin and moan, and you haven't seen him spit in my face yet!"

But he doesn't spit. He winds his fingers through his brown baby locks, tight as can be, and pulls, pulls, screams, and pulls some more. Mrs. Latvia's eyes widen:

"Well, that's new!"

He tears out his hair in great fistfuls, his wrists taut and white from the effort, as brown curls pile up on the floor, and the baker grabs the Campbell boy and locks him in his grip. Angelina White appears to be getting her money's worth and looks like she's on the verge of fishing a butterscotch out of her purse, as if she were at the movies, only under the circumstances it would be improper.

"Samuel Campbell, listen to Latvia, listen to your Latvia!"

The child sobs silently, his hair strewn about the floor, someone's going to have to sweep it all up. If his late mother the hairdresser could see the mess and the state of her son's scalp, she'd turn seven times in her grave before saying a word, we swear she would.

Mrs. Latvia sits him on a chair and kneels before him:

"Did you come here alone, Samuel Campbell? Where is Blanche Bedford?"

The strange child says nothing, and from our viewpoint, we can only see his back, but he seems to be showing something to the florist, and she stands up, as white as a funeral wreath.

The baker grimaces and shouts out:

"Where is that Bedford girl? Why is she afraid to show herself here? Why did she send the child?"

Mrs. Latvia, her face as pale as if she'd just seen one of her holy visions, shouts:

"Quiet!"

We jump. Despite her venerable age and her wrath, the florist has never displayed such impoliteness, and why is she so pale, what did the Campbell child show her? Mr. Leaven steps forward and takes the boy by the arm, then lets him go just as quickly, a mystified look on his face, one we've never seen on him before:

"What's that on his sleeve?"

We can't contain ourselves any longer; we get up and walk toward the Campbell boy. If they won't tell us, we'll just have to see for ourself what has them looking so dazed, we take Samuel's arm and ahhh! his sleeve!

His sleeve, stained red.

But perhaps he ate a jelly doughnut, perhaps he got some on his shirt? Perhaps it's something else?

The baker motions to Dr. Harmer, who examines the stain—what can he possibly tell with those eyes that have seen pharaohs, the fall of two empires, and three revolutions, but since the baker still appears to have faith in him, we keep quiet—and confirms out loud what all are thinking.

"Do you think...?"

Angelina White is certainly getting bolder:

"Do you think something has happened to Blanche?"

Angelina White looks at Mrs. Latvia, who looks at Baker Leaven, who looks at Doctor Harmer, who looks at Father Wavery, who scratches his knee. You could hear a pin drop if it weren't for the doctor wheezing from his asthma and all those brains whirring a mile a minute, including ours, but what should we do, what should we do, if we're going to do something it will mean interrupting the meeting, but that's never been done before, at least not as far back as we can remember.

The baker snaps us out of our reverie by jumping up and charging, yes, charging, to the sacristy staircase! And everyone in the room, including us, runs after him. There's jostling and shoving on the stairs, but we manage to get to the front of the pack. Leaven, it must be said, is not the swiftest of bakers. Once we're in the church, we tear down the aisle at high speed and careen to a halt in front of the main door.

There's a cold wind blowing outside and it whistles through the cracks and into the house of God. The others soon crowd around behind us. The baker calls out:

"Well, are you going to open that door or not?"

We turn to look at him. We don't say a word; we just block the doorway. The baker is clearly losing patience:

"Open the door or move aside! A woman's life could depend on it!"

Always the loud mouth, always his booming voice, the baker almost has us convinced, but we stand our ground, our feet firmly planted.

"I said 'Move aside.'"

And he tries to shove us out of the way, what a boor, that Leaven, but nothing is going to make us move aside, nothing can stop us from being there, just being there, in front of this church door, and the baker finally realizes it:

"What's going on? Are you refusing to let us go to Blanche's aid? Are you refusing to let us leave the church?"

We don't speak, we just stand there. Anyway, even if we tried, we're quite sure we would stay right there, in this church, in front of this heavy door. That's just the way things have to be, and it's here they have to happen. Mrs. Latvia and Father Wavery cross themselves, the baker narrows his eyes, grits his teeth, curses us, and returns to the basement with the others.

When we're sure they've all gone downstairs, we go back up the aisle and head down beneath the sacristy once again.

12

ON FRIDAY, *we* wait, we wait, we wait in the church basement. But the Professor doesn't come to us. We fret, we brood, we sweat a lot, and we finally go home, empty-handed, lost.

13

WE REALLY DON'T KNOW WHERE TO BEGIN. This has been the most extraordinary week the village has ever known.

First, Monday's meeting ended on a morose note: Leaven sulked and shot baleful glances at us for the rest of the evening, while Mrs. Latvia tried without success to get Samuel Campbell to talk. Angelina White eventually found a broom in the closet and proceeded to sweep up the clumps of hair from the floor while whistling an inappropriately chirpy melody.

In the end, since it was getting late and we were all exhausted, we drifted home. As it turns out, Blanche Bedford had disappeared. It was Mrs. Latvia who made the discovery that same evening, then told Angelina White, who repeated it to everyone else: the Campbell kids had found their own way to Mrs. Latvia's house, where she greeted them with a twinge of bitterness and a plate of jelly doughnuts before going to knock on Blanche's door.

But there was no Blanche, no Albert, no anyone, no explanation, and they'd taken nothing with them. All of their belongings were still there, intact. As Mrs. Latvia would say: there's trouble in Tulipland.

And then there's Amelia. The poor child succumbed to her suffering, she did, and now the whole village is grieving. Even Sybille came to pay her last respects, apparently she was crying. Sybille with tears running down her chapped cheeks, now *there*'s a sight we've never seen. It takes a lot to hurt her feelings, otherwise she would surely melt into a puddle every time the baker spits at her feet. Mrs. Latvia heard it from Angelina White that Sybille kept talking about a prophecy—her and her sorceress ways... In another age she would have been burned at the stake.

Mayor Gross is absent, as is Morosity, and in their absence, Father Wavery decides to address the gathering before the baker jumps in, a rare occurrence indeed:

"My dear flock, Roger and Morosity Gross have asked me to pass on a message to you."

Not surprising, given the circumstances, they probably want to enlighten us a bit, after all we've been in the dark all week long, what with Mrs. Latvia who's taken back the Campbell children, Blanche and Albert who've skedaddled, and Amelia, ahhh, poor Amelia...

"As you know, their dear Amelia joined her Creator on high this week—Amen."

Dr. Harmer's shoulders tremble. His nerves seem to have gotten the better of him; at his age he should be reading the paper and smoking a pipe, not working and running the risk of having his medical licence revoked for causing a teenage girl to bleed to death. The priest continues:

"Roger and Morosity found an envelope in their daughter's things dated the day of her death and addressed to the entire village. What a blessing that she should be so lucid at the end to send us one last prayer! The Lord must have left her enough strength to accomplish this final task—Amen."

He's going a bit overboard with his blessing this and Lord that, but we're not going to contradict him. The baker might have, were he not so busy glaring at us: he still hasn't digested the unexplained disappearance of Blanche and Albert, and he clearly blames us. The fact remains, the blood on Samuel's sleeve still hasn't been identified. Enigmas come and enigmas go.

The priest raises his arm, as solemn as if he were serving mass, opens the envelope, and takes out a little notebook covered in brown spots. He opens it and reads out loud:

Amelia's Diary

April 20

I turned fourteen yesterday, but I won't live to see my fifteenth birthday. And I've resigned myself to it. I'm ready. My arms are open and I'm waiting for death to take me.

It's not that I'm morbid.

But I must accept the prophecy.

(What a way to start a diary! That's exactly what we meant when we said that Amelia always spoke like she was preparing to eat her last meal. You have to wonder whether the girl was spending time with Sybille, to wax agnostic like that. The child was always a bit unusual, that is, before

106

Samuel Campbell stole the limelight with his trauma. The priest continues.)

April 23

I spoke to Sybille last night. As soon as Mom and Dad were asleep, I slipped out my window and followed the light into the forest. I'm not scared in the woods, despite the wild animals and all the stories about evil spirits. That's just nonsense made up to keep the Campbell kids from straying too far. Mom always says if only their mother would keep those kids under control, she wouldn't have to come up with such sordid legends.

I followed the light into the forest and found Sybille. She was sitting by the fire waiting for me, and she smiled. I don't know if she does it every evening, but she had grilled a big fish that she ate with her fingers.

She sang me some strange songs. It made a change from Mom's piano playing.

(We stir anxiously. So Sybille *is* mixed up in this prophecy business, and all she had to do was plant the idea in poor Amelia's head for the girl to take it as the gospel truth. All these revelations are sending our head spinning! The baker looks perturbed too, and Mrs. Latvia, as always, is teary-eyed and sniffly. Even Father Wavery, apparently still touched by the blessing, pulls out a handkerchief to blot his holy tears before reading on.)

May 2

It's Friday, and Dad and Mom have gone off to one of their meetings again. Sometimes this village is so boring. But I have a feeling something is going to happen. Perhaps I'm going to die. If I had the choice, I don't know who I would rather have for a mother—Mom or Mrs. Latvia.

(The poor child must have been terribly confused to imagine that our meetings took place on Fridays instead of Mondays. Mrs. Latvia points it out to the priest, who nods gravely and lowers his gaze to the notebook.)

May 10

Father Wavery picks a peck of pickled pepper. Actually, he picks his nose when he thinks no one is watching.

(Hah, we don't need anyone's diary to tell us that, you only have to attend Sunday mass, but still, the girl had gall, and a touch of literary flair too, and now the priest blushes, we're willing to bet he'll be keeping his fingers well away from his nostrils for the next few weeks.)

May 11

Dear Diary,

Dad told me that, last night, the baker accused Sybille of stealing his bread. I doubt it's true: Sybille only eats what the forest offers up.

Mom is playing her sad tune on the piano again. I sometimes feel like slamming the lid on her fingers.

They say Blanche Bedford is going to marry Albert Miller. Anyway, those two are going straight to hell—I saw them fornicating in the cemetery one night. She's already fat as it is.

(How mortifying for Blanche and Albert. If only they had been here, Leaven might have left us alone for a moment to turn his inquisitorial gaze on them instead, and what about Morosity Gross, aside from the fact it's true she always plays the same melody on the piano, to the point

109

we suspect it's the only one she knows, and in fact it has occurred to us that perhaps it's a pianola with a little mechanism that repeats the same tune over and over.)

May 13

Dear Diary,

Aunt Albania came to see me this morning. It's awful what she's going through. You know her thyroid is like an old lady's? I don't know exactly what a thyroid is, but hers is in worse shape than Mrs. Latvia's.

She showed me her potions and pick-me-ups and tonics. She even told me some of them would probably help perk me up.

She talked for a long time about the baker, who she suspects of something, I'm not quite sure what.

Dad has always said that Aunt Albania loves me so much she'd go to hell and back for me. Personally, I'm not sure Aunt Albania loves anyone aside from herself.

(Clearly, young Amelia was the most lucid member of the family. We glance around the room, there's no sign of Albania, who must be utterly devastated by the death of her niece, or at least pretending to be. We imagine her sprawled across her huge bed, a photo of Amelia in her hand, her face all puffy, her thyroid causing her more trouble than ever...)

May 18

Dear Diary,

Dad has asked Dr. Harmer to remove my wisdom teeth. I don't care one way or another, to tell you the truth, but they seem to think it's important.

And while we're on the subject of the doctor, I have to tell you something: once, while I was waiting in his waiting room, I opened the door of his office a sliver—I was alone—and saw him in there. You'll never guess, dear Diary, what he was doing! He was plucking licorice candies out of a little metal box, unwrapping them and stuffing them into his mouth while staring off into space. Then, he would smooth out the wrappers and put them back in the box. And he would keep on doing the same thing. While I had been waiting for a whole hour! I swear, dear Diary, I saw him polish off one candy after another for a good ten minutes, then he put away the box, straightened his tie, stood up—that's when I closed the door—and called me into his office.

I think Dr. Harmer eats way too many candies for a man his age, but I think he does it because he has nothing else to look forward to in life.

Hmm, maybe I should try licorice candies too.

(We turn to Harmer, but he's looking elsewhere. Mrs. Latvia says:

"How strange, this story about licorice candies. Lisa Campbell used to do the same thing—that box full of carefully folded candy wrappers I found in her desk..."

We don't think anything of it, after all, there are surely many of us in the village who enjoy licorice drops and their pretty wrappers, so colourful that it's perfectly normal to want to hang onto them to admire them at our leisure.)

May 20

Dear Diary,

Yesterday the doctor took out my wisdom teeth. But he's so clumsy he hurt me with his pliers. He told me it was nothing serious and that my recovery would just be a bit longer. Now I have a terrible headache, and everything I try to swallow tastes like metal.

Sybille came to visit me while Mom was out running errands. Judging by how she reacted when she saw me, I suspect I've looked better.

I've been resting a lot and staying in bed.

May 25

I don't know how truthful they're being. My teeth hurt worse than ever. The doctor has been giving me one injection after another, but they don't seem to make any difference. I spit up red and white into my basin several times a day.

Mom plays her sad song on the piano all the time. Dad is stuttering more than usual.

Last night the doctor sat by my bedside until the early morning. I swear it was like I was on my deathbed. And the worst thing is he sat there eating his licorice candies all night long without offering me a single one.

(That was rather selfish of our doctor, while poor Amelia could have enjoyed one last opportunity to savour one of those delicious sweets— just the thought of it makes us salivate. The doctor protests:

"I was sure she was sleeping! I wasn't going to wake her up to offer her a candy."

He has a point, but still, it seems a bit cruel, especially for a doctor—and an old man, at that.)

June 1

What if the prophecy were being fulfilled? Is this how I'm going to die? What a stupid way to die! Mind you, Sybille never told me how I was going to die. Still, I would have preferred to die like Lisa Campbell, shot dead by a hunter's bullet. It's much more romantic. And prophetic too, it seems to me.

I can't write for much longer. I get tired so fast.

(What has Sybille gone and made up again to manipulate Amelia with her prophecy nonsense? The priest looks skeptical too, then continues reading.)

June 7

Dear Diary,

No one says anything about it to me, but I can see the way Mom winces every time she comes in the room. Doctor Harmer doesn't even bother coming by anymore. Or maybe he's just dropped dead of old age or guilt, and they've decided to spare me the news.

It hurts so much it's almost like it doesn't hurt at all.

Earlier today Samuel Campbell snuck in through my window. I hadn't seen him for ages. He's getting to be quite handsome, but he seems to have a few screws loose. He didn't say a word, even when I said hello, but he came over to my bed. The idiot wasn't paying attention and stained his sleeve in my basin.

I asked him what he was up to outside on his own. I don't know how Blanche Bedford is raising him, but she doesn't appear to be any better at it than Mrs. Latvia.

He handed me a little scrap of paper. This is what was written on it:

"Dear little Amelia,

Forgive me for not coming to see you during your convalescence. You've probably heard that Albert and I are now looking after Lisa Campbell's children. It's a lot of work, and I don't have much time for anything else. (Does she really think I'm going to believe that? Mom always says that Blanche spends her days dilly-dallying at the mill with Albert while Mrs. Latvia frets about the children being left on their own.) The reason I'm writing to you this evening is to let you know that Albert and I are moving to the city. The baker can go mill his own flour.

I trust this note finds its way to you.
Get well soon,
Blanche"

Father Wavery looks up at the ceiling, either to be closer to God, or to watch the spider rappelling down toward his nose.

"And it appears there's a brief epilogue, at the end of the diary. It's very short:

Someone has certainly killed me.
Then slipped away.
On tiptoe.

That's it. The diary stops there."

The baker bristles and shouts:

"That takes the cake! Really. That evil child—God rest her soul—daring to say I wrongly accused Sybille. The old witch obviously had her wrapped around her little finger. And now Albert's gone and disappeared, leaving me all alone to manage the mill, I tell you. What a generation: ungrateful little sods!"

We don't dare point out to Leaven that, in fact, the passage in the diary is the least of our problems, sure enough, he glares straight at us when he says "ungrateful little sods!" as if we had anything to do with it, really, our baker is sinking further into ridicule with every passing day, and we can tell you, if he runs for election, we won't be voting for him, we'd rather elect Angelina White, even if her platform would likely revolve around the knitting bee. The priest clasps his hands together:

"My children, I would like to bring your attention to the epilogue I just read to you. It seems to me I've seen these same words somewhere before. In another book. And yet it's not a passage from the Bible; the scriptures make no mention of wisdom teeth. Does anyone have any idea?"

Cantarini jumps up and shouts:

"Dante! Dante!"

You can take Cantarini out of Italy, but you can't take Italy out of Cantarini, him and his Dante—he must have brought up Dante a thousand times since we've known him, Mrs. Latvia shushes him and addresses us:

"I've read it somewhere too. It's quite obvious, the girl must have copied it from a book lying around the house. All we have to do is ask Roger or Morosity."

Logical enough, but even if she had copied the passage, she must have done so intentionally, to say something, but what? Mrs. Latvia, who's never afraid to get her feet wet, raises the question:

"What could the child possibly have been trying to say with such grown-up words?"

And the baker replies:

"Obviously, she's telling us that someone killed her. Really, Mrs. Latvia. Use your common sense."

Ahh, the florist and her idiotic questions—we'd laugh if it weren't so entirely inappropriate, but in any case, the child clearly showed signs of psychological instability—we would never tell her parents, but perhaps, yes perhaps, it's just as well for them that Amelia is dead and buried.

14

TWO WEEKS WITH NO SIGN of our Professor! *We* have never experienced such agony. It has taken all our courage and patience to endure the wait, especially with everything that's been happening in the village lately. We study the others. Wherever we look, we see worried members. Will the Professor show? Will he stand us up? We perspire heavily, the lady in front of us has beads of cold sweat on the back of her neck, poor old thing.

There he is!

Before us, on the stage. He has appeared—once again—out of thin air. A sense of relief fills the hall, we jump to our feet and break out in thunderous applause. Some pull out handkerchiefs, what emotion, what a feeling of reunion. He is radiant. His cheeks are pink, with joy, no doubt. His little gold-rimmed spectacles tremble on the tip of his nose. He laughs loudly.

"My friends!"

A clamour arises... and his voice warms our hearts, after two weeks without hearing it.

"My friends! What a joy to be here with you again this evening. Because, as you probably noticed, I wasn't here last Friday."

How could we not have noticed, he's teasing us, our brilliant leader.

"That's right, I took some time out for myself. To reflect on what comes next. Whether we like it or not, my friends, we're in for a fight. Me, for the survival of our group. For the future of our meetings. You, for the survival of your Professor."

We're shocked. The survival of the Professor? Who would threaten him? Who would want to harm him? We would never let anyone do that.

"Last Monday they read the diary of the deceased girl. And someone—yes, an enemy of this group, it goes without saying—falsified the document. That's right, someone forged a passage in the diary! The epilogue, to be precise, was written *after* the child's death. Her parents swore it to me; it's not their daughter's handwriting. Someone took it upon themselves to add these words at the very end of the diary:

Someone has certainly killed me.
Then slipped away.
On tiptoe."

Whatever could it mean? We eye each other, we suspect each other, who would want to insinuate that the child was murdered? And why the mysterious style? Who in the village writes that way? So many questions our Professor attempts to answer:

"For now, I'm as much in the dark as you, my dear flock. One thing is sure: whoever this forger is, they must be an enemy of the deceased's family to spread such vile accusations. Who would dare torment two grief-stricken parents in such a way? It's shameful! It was simply bad luck and the clumsiness of a poor man too old to be working as much as he does, yet still as devoted as ever."

His gold-rimmed spectacles begin to fog up.

"Whoever came up with this nonsense shall be punished, I promise you! We do not slander others without proof, I will not allow it!"

He dismisses us with a wave of his hand, his nose bright red, and as we're filing out of the hall, we hear him in the distance repeating:

"An accident, yes. That's what it was, an accident. No one must know. An accident. The end of the diary was forged. No one will know."

15

MONDAY MARKS THE RETURN of Mayor Gross and his wife to our meetings, not that we really missed them, but after all, it's the mayor's duty to take part in the village's political life, and we presume that Morosity didn't have the courage to stay home alone in their empty house playing her depressing tune on the piano again, because she's here with her husband. A real bourgeois couple, that's what they are, him with his bow-tie and her with her wedding-cake hairdo, if anything, they seem even more bourgeois since Amelia's death—fortunately they haven't brought along Albania, whose thyroid is still causing her no end of grief. As is only logical, the mayor speaks first:

"Dear friends, we would like, my wife and I, to express our happiness at being back among you tonight. We have been through a very trying time, indeed we have! A very trying time. But it's time to move on. The village has moved on, and it's time to forget. Forget the tragedy of our little Amelia, forget all the business about the unknown huntsman, let Lisa Campbell rest in peace... life goes on."

What a strange speech from a man who was so heartbroken at his daughter's funeral only last week, and even Morosity finds the strength to smile, yes, the same Morosity to whom the apothecary says he gave enough tranquilizers to knock out a horse, to keep her from throwing herself off her piano—his words—and now they're imploring us to forgive and forget, how odd, the baker seems to think so too:

"Seriously, Mr. Mayor, with all due respect, what about Sybille? What about Blanche Bedford? What about the Petition? Need I remind you that the mystery of the unknown huntsman has yet to be resolved?"

"Yes, Mr. Leaven, you're right. There are a number of pieces still missing from the puzzle.

124

But the wave of misfortune that washed over us has now passed. Father Wavery will address this in his next sermon, I am quite sure. It's time to move forward and stop spouting the malicious talk these walls have heard in the past few weeks. The death of my daughter—God bless her soul—has broken the spell, I promise you, yes I do!"

What's our mayor playing at? Since when has he ever spoken with such self-assurance, such firmness, and without a single stutter? This about-face astounds us, it stupefies us: a hairdresser is shot dead, a bullet between her eyes, and he wants to drop the investigation, allow the damned huntsman to go free, the baker's not going to let him off that easily:

"Honestly, Mr. Mayor, are you out of your mind? The huntsman could strike again any minute! And strike anyone: he targeted Lisa Campbell, and who's to say Amelia's death was really an accident? No one here can understand how a healthy young girl could succumb to a tooth extraction. And need I remind you that she herself wrote that she was killed!"

What a nose for drama the baker has, it's all so very Greek. Mrs. Latvia, who loves a good tragedy, adds:

"The baker is right! We'll never find the murderer by burying our heads in the sand, upon my word!"

For once, we're in full agreement with the baker and Mrs. Latvia, and we almost feel like shouting it from the rooftops, but they don't need us, they're self-sustaining, if we dare say so, and we anxiously await the mayor's response:

"I've seen enough of you all. Go! Off you go home, all of you!"

Go home? What on earth has gotten into Mayor Gross? The baker, Mrs. Latvia, Angelina White, Cantarini, and the others, looking stunned, stand and make their way like robots back up to the sacristy. And we follow them, spell-bound. Troubled. The mayor removes a pair of gold-rimmed glasses from his pocket as we climb the stairs.

16

"*THEM*! They were watching me with their scheming eyes, they suspected me, yes *them*! You know who I mean by *them*, they always sit together, watching, spying, you can tell they're recording everything in their evil little minds."

The Professor hasn't kept us waiting this week, he's already pacing the hall when *we* enter. Now he's furious, our poor guru, he shouldn't get himself so worked up.

"Do you know who I'm talking about when I say *them*?"

It's us he's talking to, what an honour, we reply spontaneously, enthusiastically, without further thought, a broad smile on our lips:

"Oh yes, Professor!"

He seethes:

"Stop smiling, you morons, there's nothing funny about it. *Them*, that little group that thinks they're better than the rest, *them*, you know, those four nameless idiots who speak only with their eyes, with their gawking stares, their wandering hands on their knock knees. *Them*, they make me want to vomit."

We feel like vomiting along with him, but our stomach is empty, ahh, what a shame. There's a burning question on our lips, one we don't dare ask: Who's *them*? The Professor continues, waving his fists in the air:

"*Them*... Lucky for them they don't come to our meetings. Because if they did, let me tell you... *POW!*"

We jump. We can make out his gun by the lump in his pant pocket. Always prepared, he's all-powerful.

"It was *them* who nearly spoiled it all on Monday. When the dead girl's father agreed to let me take matters into my own hands. It's time for the village to move on. It's time to forget, yes, we must."

Take matters into his own hands—that's our leader all right—an iron fist in a velvet glove, and fox eyes looking out from behind his golden glasses.

"My friends, my lambs, desperate times call for desperate measures, isn't that so? On Monday I tried to talk sense into all those imbeciles who want to complicate things unnecessarily. But the idiots seem immune to my charisma, damn them all, I say! And then as I told you, there's *them* plotting and bad-mouthing, what a nuisance! We need to eliminate them, get rid of them. But most of all, yes most of all, we need to stop talking about the girl. It's time to move forward, to move on to other things. To put this story of the unknown huntsman to rest once and for all. And anyway, who's to say *they* are not the huntsman? What makes *them* all so sure the unknown huntsman is a single person? Couldn't it be that accursed little group? I can well imagine *them* making a pact with death to achieve their ends, believe you me!"

We jump to our feet, we break into finger-stinging applause, all for our Professor. We feel like shouting "All for you, Professor!" but that would be pure youthful folly. He bows humbly:

"Out of my sight, you drudges."

Ahh, Professor!

17

IT'S HOT THIS WEEK in the church basement, and not just because the warm days of June have arrived—prompting Sybille to break out her summer attire: now she wraps herself in kilometres of jute (her lightweight summer wear)—no, it's stifling hot in here because Angelina White, despite the woolen wraps she dons every morning, is sitting, as always, next to the woodstove, which she stuffs full of twigs every ten minutes and, quite frankly, her old bones can't possibly be still feeling the cold, and even the baker seems in agreement with us:

"For God's sake, Angelina, it's absolutely ridiculous stoking the stove like that in the middle of June—have you ever seen such a thing?"

Angelina White retreats, embarrassed, into her layers of clothing, her chignon drooping slightly, and turns to Mrs. Latvia for encouragement, but we have to agree with the baker: the meetings these days are exhausting enough without this suffocating heat to boot, ahh, there goes the mayor now:

"G-g-g-good evening, m-m-my friends. It's true the month of J-j-june has brought nice weather. And as I t-t-t-told you last week, it's b-b-best to leave the s-s-sad moments of the p-p-past few weeks behind us. I hope that each of you will do your b-b-best to m-m-move forward."

Well, well—the mayor's stutter is back with a vengeance this week, otherwise nothing new in the Gross camp, he's still got his strange habit of wanting to sweep everything under the rug, it isn't enough that Father Wavery sometimes forgets to give his Sunday sermon—the other morning, the baker had to go and drag him out of bed because the entire village was waiting in church while he slept on, something to do with communion wine, it seems—we really have no need for an elected official who buries his head in the sand, but he's off again:

"D-d-d-on't think for a m-m-minute I've forgotten my d-d-dear sweet Amelia..."

Morosity Gross, who appears to have rediscovered the will to live since last week, if her exotic hat is any indication, nonetheless cries a crocodile tear in agreement with her spouse, who looks at her, eyebrows raised, before carrying on:

"B-b-but this village cannot c-c-c-continue to live in f-f-fear. This is p-p-precisely what the unknown huntsman wants. Fear and p-p-panic that scatters our senses, c-c-c-louds our judgment, that's all he wants, it's quite obvious."

He seems quite sure of himself, our mayor, but really, what could he possibly know about the psychology of the lunatic killer on the loose, we can sense the perplexed looks of those around us, and it's good because even Angelina White has forgotten her woodstove for a moment and is wearing a look of suspicion and, of course, the baker dives right in:

"Mr. Mayor, with all due respect, I must warn you that the village has been asking itself some serious questions since last week. Can you really just brush aside the numerous tragedies that have hit our villagers in recent months and clear the slate on your own child's murder? Allow a predator like the unknown huntsman to roam unchecked? I'm not trying to pick a quarrel with you, you know, but that would be reason enough to have you relieved of your duties, Mr. Mayor, again, with all due respect."

Relieve Mayor Gross of his duties! The baker isn't pulling any punches, we know full well who he would like to see in the mayor's place, and we can assure you it's not Mrs. Latvia.

"M-m-mister Leaven, I haven't seen you consult anyone else during the meeting, therefore I c-c-cannot conclude that what you're p-p-putting forth is the result of a valid and verifiable d-d-democratic vote."

He's got a bit more verve about him now, our mayor, especially up against the baker, and if he keeps it up, he may well grow as brazen as the newly departed Blanche. For now, the baker grunts and snorts like a buffalo, perhaps he's preparing to charge, but no, he simply scowls and crosses his arms, and Mrs. Latvia takes her turn:

"Mr. Mayor."

Our florist's voice is hoarse, she must have exhausted herself looking after the Campbell kids, it's true the oldest boy still hasn't recovered the nighttime habits of a normal human being. We sometimes hear him wailing at night, his little curly-haired head visible in Mrs. Latvia's window, and that surely hasn't helped the poor old woman's sleep.

"Mr. Mayor, you're talking nonsense."

Well, she doesn't beat around the bush, does she? We sink down in our seats, even the baker's eyes widen—for once he must be feeling a little less alone—and Angelina White gathers her scrawny self and adds another stick to the fire, what an annoying habit.

"You're talking utter nonsense. We must find the unknown huntsman. If only for my own mental well-being. Oh, I know, no one gives a hoot about old Latvia, but the fact remains she's the one who looks after the three little ones all day long and, God knows, their days are long indeed."

We'd probably feel sorry for Mrs. Latvia if she didn't lay it on so thick.

"The other night the eldest snuck out of bed and went into my shop, where he ruined all my bouquets, going at them with a pair of secateurs! At least twenty bouquets, I'm not exaggerating! All that work out the window! There goes Latvia's money, straight into the garbage! I don't need to tell you I spent a terrible day cleaning the mess and redoing everything, not to mention that I couldn't see a thing through my tears. What have I ever done to the Good Lord to deserve this?"

Out comes the hankie, here come the sniffles, you know the routine and so do we. Only Angelina White still has any sympathy for our florist, rubbing her back with one hand while, with the other, she feeds a twig into the woodstove where it shrivels and curls up, like a spider crossing its legs, before being consumed by the fire.

"Miss White, enough already with the fire!"

Even Father Wavery has lost his patience—that's saying something—and Giorgio Cantarini clucks his tongue and crosses his arms, what a strange meeting, what suffocating heat, what strange times, my friends, we murmur all together, what strange times, my friends: only two months ago we were considering a simple bread theft and now here we are, sweating profusely and in distress. The glow from the ceiling light flickers, like when you stare too long at a candle flame, and everything around us shimmers in a haze, it's as if Angelina has thrown the entire church into the blaze. Fortunately the baker brings us back to our senses:

"For crying out loud, that fire is unbearable! We've got to get out of here. Have you lost your mind, my poor Angelina? I could bake my baguettes right on the floor."

And he stands up, turns his piercing gaze on us as if to say "This time you won't stop me from leaving." What dramatic flair! We follow him, and only Angelina White remains, prostrate before her woodstove, she's not in her right mind, that woman, anyway Mrs. Latvia can look after her—she's got nothing else to do, the layabout.

18

THE PROFESSOR IS ALREADY there waiting for us, standing on his pedestal. He paces nervously, as he has at every meeting since the whole unknown huntsman affair began haunting him, but really, *we*'re just speculating: we would never dare claim to understand the psychology of our guide.

We look around us. Everywhere, necks crane. Toward the sacristy stairs.

"Pardon me. I'm looking for the village officeholder."

We can't believe our eyes. Or our ears. Who is this gawker? A man. Long brown coat, khaki rain boots, chunky black plastic glasses perched askew on the end of his nose, a leather briefcase under his arm. He repeats:

"I'm looking for the officeholder."

We turn to the Professor. The officeholder? The village officeholder? We can't make head nor tail of it, nor any sense at all, for that matter. Our master adjusts his gold-rimmed glasses, squints, and, in a voice more shout than question, demands:

"Who are *you*? And what's this officeholder nonsense you're going on about?"

The stranger clears his throat, wipes a drop of rain from his cheek:

"This village must surely hold democratic elections. Who's the officeholder? The person who represents its citizens?"

Ahh! He's talking about the mayor! What a strange way of speaking, in parables like that.

Our Professor is unfazed.

"This is a private gathering, Stranger. You are not welcome here. The village meetings are held on Mondays. Come back in three days."

The stranger scratches his chin.

"I'll just take a room at the hotel then."

The hotel. That's a good one! The Professor sets him straight:

"There *is* no hotel here. Out of my sight, you miserable creature!"

The Stranger's eyebrows shoot up and his gaunt face twists into the expression of someone attempting to look smarter than everyone else.

"Oh, I'm sure I'll find somewhere to stay. I have a job to do. Have a good evening, ladies and gentlemen."

He climbs the stairs, slowly but surely, a puddle from his soaked coat the only sign he was ever there.

The Professor frowns.

"More trouble, oh yes, there's more trouble in store. Perhaps I should have gotten rid of that meddler right away. Oh, what have I done... well, he's gone now. Trouble, my children, there's trouble in store, I'm telling you!"

If you say so, Professor.

19

WE HAVEN'T SLEPT SINCE SATURDAY, we've been so excited by the arrival of a stranger, an odd sort of city mouse lost in the country. At first we thought—oh joy!—he was a constable come to re-establish order, drawn by some rumour carried on the wind all the way to the gates of the city, but word quickly spread that he was nothing more than a scientist. His oversized glasses made quite an impression on Mrs. Latvia, who likened them to those worn by a German philosopher, no doubt one from the Stone Age, and Angelina White, whose door he knocked on asking for a place to stay, seems to have traded her usual rags for corseted gowns with all the requisite whalebone and tulle to resemble a lady from a great city. Farmer McDonald, who works night and day on the farm and rarely ventures into the village, spotted her near the woods picking periwinkle and daisies for her corsage, if you can believe it! We wouldn't be surprised if the stranger whisked her off her feet into a life of debauchery, poor Angelina, she's been waiting for her Prince Charming for centuries.

But Baker Leaven has no time for such nonsense, he's never been one for modesty, except in Mayor Gross's dreams, and he's certainly not afraid to show it:

"Mr. Mayor, with all due respect, I believe I speak on behalf of my fellow citizens when I ask that you allow our Guest to speak. After all, 'tis a rare occasion..."

We have to agree with him there, it is rare indeed, just ask Sybille—she was there when they decided to build the road to the village—she'll tell you: They decided the road would go no further just to isolate us, we swear it's true, because when you live at the end of the road, squeezed up against the forest like a chain-link fence, it sure makes you feel like you live in the middle of nowhere. Now the Guest is getting to his feet. He's wearing a grey suit, his hair slicked back as if he's at Sunday mass, doing his best to appear serious:

"Good evening, everyone."

He smiles at us, and we return the nice Guest's smile, then Angelina White stands and speaks, the shiny soles of her shoes clacking on the floor, startling Cantarini, who had nodded off, he must have been dreaming about his native Trieste or his dearly departed Nicoletta:

"Mr. Guest is actually Mr. Census-taker."

Angelina the old spinster is looking pleased as punch, she's just said more words in one minute than we've heard from her all month, but it takes more than that to impress the baker, who crosses his arms and says:

"The Census-taker? And what exactly is he sensing here?"

The stranger raises his eyebrows, lowers his eyelids, puckers his brows, widens his eyelids again, appearing to delve deep into his thoughts before replying:

"I'm conducting a census!"

Ahh, he's conducting a census, so that's it, duly noted, thank you for the clarification, Stranger. We turn to Mayor Gross who, despite his limited talents as a public speaker, did in fact pursue an education somewhere, at some time or other, and has some understanding of science, or at least that's what Morosity used to say at the late Lisa Campbell's hair salon, and he says:

"The science of census-t-t-t-aking. B-b-b-brilliant."

Well, at least there's one of us who knows what he's going on about, even Mrs. Latvia is looking disoriented, she hasn't pulled out her wretched hankies and gone all weepy on us yet, but it's only a matter of time. Fortunately the Census-taker sets the record straight:

"The science of statistics."

There he goes contradicting the mayor, oh these city folk aren't afraid of anything, we're telling you, and now the dynamics of the meeting have suddenly changed and here we are, a room full of pupils hanging on every word of a master who licks his lips and announces:

"I've been sent by the government."

We shudder. The government. It doesn't get any higher up than that, any more official, we can assure you, and just knowing the government has a vague idea of our existence sets our stomach churning and our mind spinning.

"The government needs to know exactly who lives here. Their age, their profession, more importantly, how many there are, and most important of all, their names."

That's a lot of details, a lot of information for one man, even for a Census-taker, and we swallow nervously because, frankly, exhibitionism has never been our thing. Oh sure, there was the time Amelia Gross, flanked by that homely Bertha, decided it would be nice to paint a mural on the municipal office depicting each inhabitant of the village, but she ran up against fierce opposition not only from us, but from the priest, Mrs. Latvia, the baker, practically everyone. Only Lisa Campbell, if we recall, thought it was a good idea. And Sybille, of course. So you see, when it comes to censuses and lists, well...

"I shall proceed methodically. I'm told the inhabitants of this village meet twice a week, on Mondays and Fridays."

What's this nitwit talking about? We meet on Mondays, never on Fridays, someone should set him straight, already making mistakes, it takes a government official to be so wide of the mark, how pathetic, and Leaven doesn't hold back:

"With all due respect, you are mistaken. We hold our meetings every Monday. That's it."

The Census-taker looks the baker up and down, duly noting his belly, it seems, and replies:

"Name? Age? Profession?"

The baker folds his arms and grunts:

"Beg your pardon?"

"I don't have a lot of time. We may as well get started. Name? Age? Profession?"

The room goes still, except for Angelina White, who helps herself to a licorice from her handbag as we stare wide-eyed, waiting for the baker to respond.

"If you think a fool like you is going to lay down the law in my village, you'd better think again."

Impressive. The baker's finally letting loose and speaking as if he were the one sitting in the mayor's chair, while Roger Gross, like us, passively observes the joust. He doesn't even flinch at the baker's arrogance. But the Census-taker isn't distracted:

"Name? Age? Profession?"

Leaven knits his brow as he does every time he's exhausted all his arguments, and folds his hands over his belly, then Mrs. Latvia stands:

"You don't want to get on your high horse now, Mr. Census-taker, because there are some in this village who would put you in your place in a wink."

"I'm certainly not on my high horse. I have a job to do and no one is going to stop me from doing it. This is a National Census."

There's no mistaking the capital N and the capital C, just like when the baker kept going on about his damned Petition, they take themselves so seriously, those two, and in another context they'd likely become best of friends, but now Mrs. Latvia chips in again:

"In any case, Mr. Census-taker, there are some who are not at the meeting. There are the children, and a few adults too, out of malice."

"I'm aware of that, miss."

Ahh, now it's miss, is it? Flattery will get him everywhere, and the florist softens at the sign of respect, fifty years of worry lines dropping from her forehead, but the Census-taker continues in a serious voice:

"I am aware of that. But by attending the Monday and Friday meetings, I will certainly manage to collect nearly all the information I need. As for the children, nothing could be easier; I'll go to the school tomorrow morning."

He must be a bit thick, this Stranger, going on about his Friday meeting, perhaps Angelina White served him one too many liqueurs and they went to his head, and now it's Mayor Gross who sets the Census-taker straight:

"My dear friend, you are m-m-m-mistaken. As M-m-mister Leaven m-m-mentioned, our village meetings are on M-m-m-mondays only."

The Census-taker stiffens and adjusts his hat, like a detective in the movies, before answering:

"Well then, it must have been an extraordinary meeting."

The baker and Mrs. Latvia mutter something, the mayor and Father Wavery cross themselves, and we shrug. What on earth is this fellow going on about? We almost feel like getting up and asking him, but it's Roger Gross who addresses him:

"What *is* extraordinary, my d-dear Census-taker, is your obstinacy. B-but since it's getting late, this meeting is adjourned. You will have to go about your b-b-business next week."

"No, no no! Next week, and then what? I have to be gone by Friday, at the latest."

"Mayor Gross said next week, Stranger. Surely you're not going to contradict our mayor?"

The baker oozes condescension, actually it quite suits him, and it seems to work, because the Census-taker lifts his chin and his Adam's apple glides up and down a few times like an elevator.

We leave the hall, our feet dragging, our steps heavy, eyeing the stranger who swings his arms as he walks, looking nonchalant and sure of himself, despite everything, and Cantarini, the old man who's not afraid of anything, goes up to him, no doubt to invite him for a drink at Old Man George's tavern, but the stranger strikes us as anything but the kind of man who drinks for no special reason.

20

THE PROFESSOR CHEWS on the insides of his cheeks, pressing on them with his knuckles. It's the first time *we*'ve seen him do it, and it worries us. He stares off somewhere in the foggy distance and constantly pushes his gold-rimmed glasses up to the bridge of his nose.

We know the reason for his torment; we're looking at it. The Stranger, the one who interrupted our meeting last Friday, at risk to his life, has come back to bother us again this week. This schemer is either incredibly brave or a complete and utter fool. Because to come back and taunt the Professor, he's got to be both brave and a fool.

"Stranger, what are you doing here?"

The Professor has adopted his bad-week tone, the bad weeks of smoking gun and corpses to be stepped over.

"I've come to conduct the census."

Ahh, so our new friend wants to play charades, well, he's about to find out that the Professor always wins at every game.

"No need. No use. Nobody here needs to be sensed."

"This is a Mandatory National Census," the Stranger fires back just like that, and it seems to catch our master off guard, but only for a second.

"Nonsense! No one asked for a census. Go back where you came from, Intruder."

The Stranger cocks his head, crosses his arms over his big notepad, and scans the room.

"Who are you? What is this group? Why do you meet here?"

The Professor's left hand trembles, he rummages in his jacket pocket, clears his throat, and retorts in a hoarse voice:

"We have every right to be here!"

"I never said you didn't. I'm asking you what you are doing here, again, on a Friday. Are your Monday meetings not enough? Do you still have matters to discuss?"

We hold our breath. The Stranger is pushing it. He's really pushing it. The Professor stares at a point somewhere at the back of the room. He pats his pocket, clearly this is a very bad day. We turn around, there's nothing at the back of the room, nothing but the spectre of the unfortunate hairdresser killed in combat.

"You have no idea where you are, Intruder. You are venturing onto thin ice. Don't come back here. Stay with them. We don't want you here."

The Stranger adjusts his big glasses.

"Threats? Are you the elected official of this village, Mr. ...?"

The Professor smiles a tight little smile, squints, and says, in a more confident tone:

"Mr. Census-taker, there's a huntsman in this village. An unknown huntsman. A man—or a woman—who likes to prowl the woods in search of wild beasts. But the hunter is reckless. He shoots without warning. He's careless. His bullets tend to stray. He's struck before. And the day will come—without a shadow of a doubt—when he strikes again. It's not safe here for a stranger. Go back to your city. Follow the road, you can't miss it: it ends right here. Follow the road and go back to the city, go see the government and tell them there's nothing here. A trail that peters out at the edge of the forest, nothing more. No village. No meetings. Nothing. No one. You took a wrong turn, there was no census to be taken here. Your job is done."

The Stranger doesn't bat an eye. Instead, he lifts his chin and replies:

"Who is this huntsman? I need his name, age, and profession. Everything."

Now he's trying to be clever, well, he's going to end up caught in his own trap because, we can promise you, that charlatan doesn't stand a chance against the Professor.

"Don't say I didn't warn you, Stranger."

He sniffs loudly.

"Your job is done, Stranger."

He says it slowly, pronouncing each syllable. And we all get up and leave.

21

THIS WEEK BAKER LEAVEN announces that he's had enough:

"I've had enough!"

When a baker has had enough, which is rare because, frankly, they're all as tough as nails—or is it screws?—suffice it to say, when they've had enough, we can tell you, everyone suffers the consequences:

"I've had enough, and so has the entire village. A dead woman, okay, that's possible. Lisa Campbell, the victim of an unknown huntsman, alright, if you say so. Nobody in this village hunts, and the next town is thirty kilometres away, but who knows, maybe someone from the city decided to come flush out a pheasant or two. Next, it's decided that Amelia Gross will have her wisdom teeth out and the poor girl is butchered to death. None of it makes any sense. Then Blanche skedaddles off with her Albert, just as Mrs. Latvia is about to hand over the Campbell kids she seemed so keen on taking. And now a Census-taker who wants to lay down the law here. Seriously, Mr. Mayor, seriously my fellow citizens, seriously, this baker has had enough!"

Doctor Harmer blows his nose into his large, rough handkerchief, his eyes weepy, as always, at the mention of the girl he mutilated, and Mayor Gross and Father Wavery cross themselves in tandem. The baker, outraged as he may be, does indeed have a point: when's it all going to end? We think back with regret to last year, so peaceful, so pleasant, with the only tragedy the suicide of Mayor Morton, and we miss those quiet days of calm monotony. The baker has still had enough:

"We need to move! Look for answers! Shine a light on this business!"

Well, we're not about to contradict him, except what to do, where to begin?

"Who is the Professor?"

It's the Census-taker who pipes up, he'd been standing silently just behind us, we jump at the sound of his voice so close, and everyone in the room appears in a state of shock, but it's Mrs. Latvia who finally replies:

"The professor's name is Timothy Worne. Do you mean to say you conducted a census of the children at the school, and you don't even know the name of their teacher?"

Well said, madam florist, can you believe it, the Census-taker goes out of his way to harass our poor little children, and he doesn't even have the sense to write down the schoolteacher's name, does he think we're a bunch of idiots?

"No, I'm not talking about him. I'm talking about the Professor."

This time it's Mayor Gross who persists:

"The village schoolteacher is named T-timothy Worne, Mr. Census-taker, as Mrs. Latvia just t-told you. Now if you would be so k-kind as to leave us to our meeting, we would appreciate it."

Our mayor seems to have recovered since Amelia gave up the ghost, he used to buckle under the baker's thunder, and now he's just put a man from the city in his place, who would've thought?

"I will speak if I feel like it, Mr. Gross. As a matter of fact, I have something to say to you all."

He's a pretentious one, isn't he, he clears his throat and stands, straight and tall, in his mustard yellow overcoat, the one he had on the first day.

"I am not here to take away anything whatsoever from you. I am not here to cause you any harm. In my entire life, I have never seen—and believe me, I have travelled many a country road—such a backward, close-minded village as yours. You think I don't see you during the week when I knock on your doors and you pull the curtains closed like a bunch of cowards. You think I'm doing this job to harm you. What is it you're worried about? What is it you're frightened of? I've been here for two weeks, and the only thing I've managed to collect is the name and age of Miss White—and I won't tell you what I had to do to pry that information out of her—and the names and ages of the children, but only after literally extracting the details from their mouths by plying them with licorice drops, which for some inexplicable reason they all seem to love."

So our Angelina cracked, we should have guessed, she's been dolling herself up like a showgirl ever since she took in the Stranger, one languishing look was probably all it took to have her eating out of his hand, that's for sure, what a shame, Mrs. Latvia reaches for her hankie:

"Angelina, not you... how could you do that to us?"

"Do *what*? I'm simply gathering the information I need and I'm off! The faster you co-operate, the sooner I'll be gone. What could be so terrible about providing one's name, date of birth, and occupation?"

We wonder whether he really has any idea what he's saying, this strange Census-taker, with his mad scientist glasses and eccentric overcoat, if he thinks a city slicker is going to come identify us, make us leave our church, and line us up in the village square like a band of thieves, ask us our name, our age, list us, count us like cattle, well no thank you, and for once we're in agreement with the baker: we will not be pushed around. This Stranger is the cherry on the sundae that broke the camel's back. After everything that has plagued us this year, all we want is a return to the simple life. Mrs. Latvia appears to agree:

"All we asked is to carry on like we did before all this started. All we wanted was to meet here on Mondays to work out our little problems. We didn't need all this nonsense, all this upset. Good heavens! The Lord really is testing his Latvia, alas, poor Poland!"

And there she goes filling up her hankie. At the mention of her native Poland, the florist's tears flow ever more ardently, and old Cantarini rubs her back, he doesn't miss an opportunity, that one. The Census-taker takes up the charge again:

"Who is the Professor?"

His stupid questions are really getting on our nerves now, we clench our jaw, clench our fists, if we weren't holding ourself back we would probably already be rearranging the man's face, and needless to say, not in a nice way, and as if to drive home our point, Mayor Gross explodes:

"It's *Mr. Worne!*"

Not a single repeated consonant, goodness, he's really made progress recently, our elected official—ahh, now we sound like that damned Census-taker and, speak of the devil, here he comes jumping in again:

"I'm asking you who the Professor is. Not the schoolteacher. The Professor. The other elected official. The Professor."

The other elected official? If we'd known we needed to elect two mayors, we would've voted for Leaven, too, at the same time, no one ever tells us anything in this village, but we're not the only ones looking stunned: Leaven himself is lost. He raises his arms, a momentary pacifist, and proclaims:

"This whole sad story is one big ball of yarn. We need to unravel it one skein at a time. We've come this far, I think it's worth listening to the Census-taker. Go on, speak. What's this business about another elected official?"

Such a wise fellow that baker, really, Roger Gross will always be a disappointment for his lack of willpower and authority, and anyway, why not listen to what this city fool has to say, perhaps he can help enlighten our village, a place that's been too long in the dark.

"Do you mean to say you don't know the Professor's identity? You're not aware of his existence? Come, come..."

This Census-taker is annoying, heaping scorn on us like that, since we asked him to speak, you'd think he could at least get straight to the point instead of treating us like the morons we're not.

"And yet... I recognize quite a few faces here that know only too well what I'm talking about. Well, since you asked, let me tell you what I have seen since I arrived in this village. The fact is that every Friday—"

"It's getting late, my children, very late. We should adjourn this meeting and all turn in, isn't that so, Mayor Gross?"

It's Father Wavery who's spoken, his forehead slick with sweat, perhaps it's getting late for him at his ripe old age, mind you there's nothing stopping him from heading for bed at the presbytery, as the baker points out. But the priest stays put and sits back down, looking a little grey around the gills, his health is obviously in decline. The baker says:

"Carry on, Census-taker."

We prick up our ears, he opens his mouth:

"The fact is that every Friday..."

22

WE HUNKER DOWN ON FRIDAY. We wait, in the dark and silence. The Professor has made it known he won't be holding a meeting. We mustn't go to the church. We mustn't make a sound. We don't know where we are. But we must not be at the church, that much is clear. We must be somewhere else.

23

THIS WEEK WE ARRIVE at the Monday meeting
with the certitude—hurray!—yes, the certitude,
the very first in weeks, months, and at last we
breathe freely because everyone knows that life
is a constant quest for certitudes that oxygenate
the brain, that's no doubt how Harmer, the old
scholar, would put it, in any case our neurons
are snapping and popping thanks to this certitude we know will be revealed tonight because
that's what certitudes do—they bring the truth
to light, the one and only, reassuring, and smug
truth. What joy to be able to finally shout it out,
loud and clear, in unison, like the hymn of a
community divided for too long by tragedy and

opprobrium—ahh, this week has recentred us so profoundly we feel awakening within us the spirit of a writer or perhaps a poet, it has confirmed once again that good always triumphs over evil—in the movies, in books, at the hair salon, and at church, and speaking of church, Father Wavery has made up his mind to speak:

"My children, this week has, once again, served us up a great divine lesson."

As usual he lays it on good and thick with the whole divinity thing, but what else would you expect from a priest, and in any case, our bliss is so immense that his holy roller speech isn't going to spoil it, and off he goes again:

"As I'm sure you know, Mayor Gross, Baker Leaven, and myself came here last Friday evening to see whether there was any truth to the Census-taker's statements about the existence of a secret gathering."

What nerve he had, that accursed Census-taker, now that we think about it! He changed his tune soon enough, he can brag all he wants about living in a city and working in the realm of officialdom in a national capacity, oh how good it feels to talk that way.

"That's right, my little ones, we came here Friday evening. And as many of you no doubt already know, we didn't find a thing. There was no one. Not a soul. Simply the invisible, eternal presence of the Father, the Son, and the Holy Spirit. Amen."

We all explode with joy, we haven't experienced such happiness for so very long, three months to be exact, even Sybille must be able to hear us deep in her forest, where perhaps she's sacrificing a mole to celebrate this blessed day, goodness we sound like Father Wavery, who hasn't said his last word:

"The Census-taker lied to us with impunity, and who knows to what end. Such a man cannot force us to submit to his census, no matter how national. The Census-taker, my friends..."

He takes a tragic pause, clutches his fist to his heart—what a theatrical priest we have—and continues:

"The Census-taker, my friends, is none other than the unknown huntsman."

At that, we erupt into applause, we stamp our feet, we drum on our bellies just for the fun of it, we whistle an airy tune—yes, all this business has ended well, extraordinarily well, at last we have found our unknown huntsman and everything can go back to being simple again! Even Father Wavery, who spends his evenings studying the cold statues in his temple so that one fine Pentecost he can turn rigid in the very same beatitude, looks like he's on the verge of allowing a single waxy tear to trickle down his hollow cheeks; we bet if we offered him a little glass of the wine he loves so well, his hands would soon cleave apart in a crack of splitting stone, and sure enough, he smiles and says:

"There is no darkness the Lord cannot light with His truth."

Well said, Father, well said. And he sits back down, his eyes glistening with modesty at what he must consider as proof of the existence of God, in the same way Mrs. Latvia's misfortunes prove it for her.

"Where is that nasty Census-taker anyway?"

Surprise, surprise. It's Angelina White who wants to know! There's a bitter twinge in her voice, we get the feeling she'd have been happy to take the census every day if she could. She's got a heart as soft as marshmallow, that's what Mrs. Latvia sometimes says behind her back, it's true, and—really!—having a crush at her age, we have to say, it's so pathetic it's almost vulgar, but now the baker picks right up where she left off:

"She's got a point. What have you done with that scoundrel? Mayor Gross? Father Wavery? Did you lock him up at the Station?"

The Station? What an idea, we'd rather spend the night in Sybille's lair than in that stone blockhouse no one ever thought to grace with a single window, as if to drive to depression the poor devils there who've sided with Evil, as if it weren't enough to deprive them of their freedom, but come to think of it if there's one person who deserves to rot there for a few days it's certainly that rogue of a Census-taker, yes, perhaps the Station is perfectly appropriate for criminals of his stripe, but we shudder when we recall that the late mayor Morton once talked about locking up Amelia Gross there for the whole pen heist affair, just to "set an example." How horrendous! Fortunately the baker would have none of it, and the Gross girl was allowed to roam free until recently when—alas!—she took her last breath and was locked away to rot in a poplar box instead. It's the priest who responds:

"Yes, the Census-taker is at the Station for now. We locked him up there—he fought like a devil, the poor sinner—and we swallowed the key, so to speak. A demon of his ilk deserves a little solitude, Amen."

We raise our eyebrows. Swallowed the key, that's going a bit far isn't it, and what a curious gift to leave to future generations—the skeleton and ghost of a census-taking monster haunting the walls of the Station for ever and ever, Amen! We sound like Father Wavery now—that's all we needed!—but the more we think of it, the less we want to know; after all, as those more intel-lectual than us might say, what we don't know makes us stronger and what doesn't kill us can't hurt us.

"Surely you're not going to let him rot there like a stack of old firewood?"

Angelina's voice carries a tremolo not unlike Morosity's when she belts out the hymns at Christmas mass, poor Angelina, she's been jinxed since birth, always dreaming of being wed while, one after another, her suitors end up in the slammer, behind bars, in the corner, or worse—at the Station. It's enough to make us cry, but we won't allow anything to soften us, we won't allow anything to distract us from our thankless but necessary task, as Leaven points out:

"With all due respect, Miss White, you have consorted with the enemy, and in another age, in another country, and in a completely different situation, you would have had your head shorn. So, spare us your scruples!"

Mrs. Latvia takes out her ridiculous hankie—does she wash the thing every Monday?—and hands it to her friend, who sheds three or four tears into it before tossing a twig into the wood-stove, and we all watch it crackle and burn up.

24

WE BREATHE EASY, yes *we* breathe easy this evening in the church basement. We are finally rid of the vermin, thanks to our brilliant Professor. And our days of peace and quiet can return.

"My flock, the terrible Stranger is no longer standing in our way. Let us thank the heavens, yes, and take a moment once again to loathe that Enemy, that Stranger, that pseudo-scientist, and let us pray for the redemption of his soul."

We clap, we have tears in our eyes. How lucky we are to have such a master, such a guide as the Professor! He rocks back on his heels, visibly pleased, and calls for silence.

"There is one step left, one last step, to ensure we all enjoy eternal peace. To end, once and for all, this damned season, this damned novel."

We can feel the cramps creeping back into our stomach and cold sweat breaking out in our armpits. We thought this season and this novel were over and done with, but no, there's one more step, one last step, ahh!

"We must incriminate that Demon once and for all. Brand him forever with a red-hot iron. So that each and every one of us remembers him as the devil who once visited our village and who was vanquished and locked up forever in the Station. He must become the unknown huntsman, beyond the shadow of a doubt."

Of course, if we could prove beyond a doubt, like they do in court, that this Stranger is in fact the unknown huntsman, then the whole thing would be resolved. But is it really necessary, Professor, can't we just let popular belief, rumour, and time do their work? Can't we just get back to our quiet lives?

"We must. So we can find peace. So I can find peace. And I have a secret weapon, oh yes, I do. Come, follow me."

He gestures to something behind us, our head swivels to understand, to watch the shadow coming down the sacristy staircase and entering the room.

And we understand!

25

OUR MEETING THIS WEEK is full of surprises again, just when we thought we were all done with surprises. As we come into the hall and sit down, who should we see there, just to the right of Father Wavery—on whose left sits Mayor Gross—sitting modestly, slightly hunched, wearing a plain cotton dress, but the young schemer Blanche Bedford.

The baker doesn't waste a second and booms, in a mocking voice:

"Well, well. Look who's back!"

The mayor—there's something different about him, but we can't put our finger on it—is not amused:

"That's enough, Leaven, that's right, now you're going to listen for a change!"

It seems this mayor stutters—or not—when it suits him! But we have to say we prefer this Gross to the other one who can barely string two words together, and now the mayor is clearly in control again:

"Blanche Bedford is back. And she's brought with her the final proof that will conclude this thing, this season, this novel, once and for all."

What flair our mayor has!

"Show them, Blanche."

Mrs. Latvia can hardly contain herself, the poor woman has had to endure the Campbell boys' nervous breakdowns since Blanche disappeared without a trace, we can tell she's exhausted, and Blanche can tell too, but young Blanche simply looks up and pulls a slip of paper from her pocket.

"The paper from Lisa Campbell's salon! I knew it! That little bitch had it the whole time, just to taunt us, just to torment us! Damn her generation! Lord, give your old Latvia strength!"

"Thank you, Mrs. Latvia, spare us your comments if you will."

Such poise from Roger Gross this evening! What ever happened to our meek and mild mayor with his mumbling, stumbling voice?

The Bedford girl unfolds the piece of paper, glances at the mayor, the priest, her audience, Mrs. Latvia, back at the mayor, and opens her precious little mouth:

James Campbell, Census-taker
Ministry of Census
Government
555-0174

And she scrutinizes the audience, looking as smug as an actress who's just delivered a diatribe.

"So that's it, then. James Campbell, brother of Bertrand Campbell, ex-husband of the late Lisa Campbell, is none other than the criminal rotting at the Station as we speak. That explains the murder of Lisa Campbell who, according to Mrs. Latvia's testimony, was carrying on a risqué relationship with him. That explains everything."

Mayor Gross enunciates every syllable as he speaks, as if to cut short any discussion, any debate, but he knows Leaven only too well, and the baker won't be silenced so easily.

"Wait a minute now, where is Albert Miller? What've you done with him, Blanche? Jilted is he, the poor boy?"

Blanche glances around as if looking for her mate, as if she'd forgotten him in a corner somewhere, the way you might misplace a handkerchief or a glove.

"Albert died at the front."

It's the mayor who's answered, and we frown. Mrs. Latvia and Angelina White stiffen and cross themselves, and even Blanche has an odd look on her face, but she chimes in:

"There's a terrible war raging."

"Really? Where?"

"In the city."

"How long has it been going on?"

"For months."

"Why have we never heard about it?"

"But Baker Leaven, we never know anything about anything. We've had only one outsider here in the past ten years, and look what happened to him."

"True, but why would the government conduct a trivial little census in the middle of a war?"

"You really don't get it, do you? James Campbell did *not* come here to carry out a census; he's nothing but a *dangerous* madman."

Now it's the mayor who's spoken, and we can see he's getting more worked up than we've ever seen him before, waving his arms around, his face the same shade as Mrs. Latvia's when she throws one of her tragic fits.

But Leaven's not giving up:

"Well then, let's call the number, now that Blanche has given it to us. We'll find out, once and for all, whether the stranger languishing at the Station is in fact James Campbell, whether he's a census-taker, and whether this affair is actually as resolved as they tell us."

He's a tough nut, that baker! But it's true this whole story has been dragging on for so long and has worn us all out so much that we may as well get to the deep dark bottom of it and call that number.

"Obviously the number will no longer be in service. All the government offices have been destroyed. The line will have been cut."

That Blanche has all the answers, but even so, Leaven snatches up the slip of paper—he's got some nerve—and rushes over to the telephone.

The mayor, the priest, and the Bedford girl stare straight ahead, what strange looks on their faces, and the baker grips the phone as if he were clutching Sybille by the neck after catching her in the act of stealing a loaf, and after a minute or so, his hand relaxes and he turns around:

"The number is no longer in service."

We let out a collective sigh, old Cantarini slips his arm around Mrs. Latvia's shoulder, and for the first time in centuries the tension that usually holds her together eases. Angelina White adjusts her shawl.

"But the fact remains we'll never really know. We'll never really get to the bottom of this whole story. Doesn't that drive you crazy?"

Leaven is talking to us all, but he may as well be talking to the wall; we're not going to answer him, enough is enough. For once, we're in full agreement with the priest and the mayor, it's time to let this season—and this story—go. Once and for all!

"Blanche, my dear, you will be so kind as to take back the Campbell children now that you appear to have returned from the dead."

Mrs. Latvia is hedging her bets, and in the presence of witnesses to boot, she's back to her usual stiff, upright self, and she jabs poor old Cantarini with a well-aimed elbow. Angelina White is the only one who still looks somewhat out of sorts, she hasn't stoked the fire once and then, in a fit of madness deserving of instant incarceration at the Station, she lets out a piercing howl.

"You locked him up! You killed him! It's *you*, the damned unknown huntsman! Jesus, Mary, Joseph, and all the saints. It's *you*, the unknown huntsman!"

And she points straight at us, at *us*, and we have no idea who she's talking about, her voice so shrill she sounds just like Albania throwing one of her tantrums, good heavens, even the baker looks stunned, the priest crosses himself with the wrong hand, and Blanche Bedford giggles—what's gotten into her?—then Angelina White continues:

"Of course *I* spoke to the Census-taker! Lord above, he is not the huntsman, may I leap into the flames and burn to a cinder if I'm not telling the truth!"

Mrs. Latvia quickly moves to stand in front of the woodstove to prevent her crazed friend from doing the irreparable, we grip our chair so tightly our knuckles turn white, and Mayor Gross replies:

"Miss White, you can be sure we have all shared the same thought at one time or another. It crossed all of our minds that it could have been them, yes! But it has been decided and proven by the priest and myself that the Census-taker is, without a doubt, the unknown huntsman. He is none other than James Campbell, the secret lover of the late Lisa Campbell who came from the city to torment us, to torture us. To have created such a stir among us, he can only be an enemy of our village! My friends, my children, I'm telling you this novel must end right now. There's no point racking our brains any longer. The light that needed to be shed on this matter has been shed. May we find peace once again."

He's got some nerve, our Mayor Gross, sharing his evil thoughts out loud like that: *us*, the unknown huntsman! It's utter nonsense, and merely further proof that this can't go on any longer, that our village is on the edge of the abyss, that we must put this whole thing to rest and be done with it, done with it for good!

The baker eyes the mayor even more dubiously, and we can tell he's on the verge of giving him a piece of his mind, but before he can, Angelina White springs out of her chair and rushes toward the sacristy staircase, completely hysterical, she reminds us of Sybille, if you could see her, screaming "Take my census!" Goodness, the woman has lost her mind, and Mrs. Latvia comes unglued, and the mayor sprints after her, and we follow them, here we go, another race up the staircase, we push, we shove, we jostle for position, Mrs. Latvia gets trampled in the process—collateral damage—and we finally make it to the nave and the aisle, and we run as fast as we can, gasping and panting, but—horror of horrors!—the others all get to the door before us, Angelina first, and now she's grasping the latch, turning the handle, pushing, opening, opening!

We close our eyes and turn back. We won't go out, no, we won't. We wait for the silence, and when it's time, we'll go back down beneath the sacristy. This can end. It must end, so be it, but as for us, we shall stay inside.

Page 116

Someone has certainly killed me.
Then slipped away.
On tiptoe.

Anne Hébert, translated by Sheila Fischman
In the Shadow of the Wind (House of Anansi
Press, 1983)

QC Fiction brings you the very best of a new generation of Quebec storytellers, sharing surprising, interesting novels in flawless English translation.

Available from QC Fiction:

LIFE IN THE COURT OF MATANE by Eric Dupont
(translated by Peter McCambridge)

THE UNKNOWN HUNTSMAN by Jean-Michel Fortier
(translated by Katherine Hastings)

Coming soon from QC Fiction:

BROTHERS by David Clerson
(translated by Katia Grubisic)

LISTENING FOR JUPITER by Pierre-Luc Landry
(translated by Arielle Aaronson and Madeleine Stratford)

BEHIND THE EYES WE MEET by Mélissa Verreault
(translated by Arielle Aaronson)

Visit **qcfiction.com** for details and to subscribe
to a full season of QC Fiction titles.

Printed in October 2016
by Gauvin Press,
Gatineau, Québec